DANNY ORLIS
and the
MODEL PLANE MYSTERY

DANNY ORLIS
and the MODEL PLANE MYSTERY

By

BERNARD PALMER

MOODY PRESS

CHICAGO

ISBN: 0-8024-7246-X

Printed in the United States of America

Contents

5

Contents

1

The Model Plane Club

GARY TRUMBO'S LEAN FRAME was cramped into the rear seat of the family VW, along with their dog, a small suitcase, and Gary's younger sister, Patti. Although he was only thirteen, he was almost as long as his dad and didn't fold up much more easily. He wasn't sure he would ever get his knees straightened out again.

Trying to ignore the ache that was going deep into his bones, he leaned forward and searched the fading western skyline for a glimpse of Rock Point, Colorado. His dad had been driving for three days since leaving the town in Ohio where they had been spending their missionary furlough. Now the family was on their way to Rock Point where Virgil Trumbo was going to take advanced training at the missionary flight school where Danny Orlis taught.

"Gary," a small voice said.

7

He turned to glance at the impish face of his
ten-year-old sister.

"Yeah," he growled. It wasn't that he didn't like
her, it was just that she bugged him all the time.

"You are going out for football this year, aren't
you?"

He groaned. He might have known it. She had
been after him all last year. Now she was starting
in again. There were times when he wished their
dad hadn't been a pro halfback. Then maybe
everybody wouldn't expect him to play the stupid
game.

"Get off my back, will you?"

Fires kindled in her eyes, and her lips tightened
angrily. "I wish I was a boy, that's what I wish."

Gary did not answer her. When she was on that
football kick, trying to talk to her only led to a
good argument, and then Mom and Dad got uptight and usually blamed him for it.

"You're the oldest. You don't have to argue with
her," they informed him.

There was no use trying to tell them how bratty
she was.

He guessed football was all right for the guys
who liked it, but it wasn't for him. What he really
wanted to do was to learn to fly. He had been interested in aircraft and becoming a pilot even before his dad began his flying lessons when they returned from the mission field for this furlough.

Now that they were moving to Rock Point, where his dad would be taking advanced instruction, Gary was ecstatic.

"Do you think I could learn to fly, Dad?" he had asked only an hour before.

"I don't see why not."

He hadn't expected anything so positive. "Can I start right away?" he asked. "When you do?"

"Now wait a minute." His dad laughed. "I said there's no reason you can't learn to fly, but I didn't say when. There'll be plenty of time for that when you get out of school, Gary. You might not even be interested by then."

He knew better than that, and said so. He had already made up his mind: flying was for him. That was what he wanted to do with his life. There wouldn't be anything better in all the world than handling the controls of a jumbo-jet or even maneuvering a Cessna 180 onto one of those short landing strips like his dad would be using.

He had been thinking about the mission field. That would be good, too, especially if he could be a missionary pilot like his dad.

"I don't see why you're so stubborn about going out for football," Patti continued. "If the folks would let me, I'd be playing."

"You!" he exploded contemptuously. "That's a laugh!"

"You think I couldn't, don't you?"

He sighed his disgust. "Just skip it, Pat. Okay?"

"If you'd just try football, you'd like it." She raised her voice. "Wouldn't he, Dad?"

"Not necessarily. One guy likes football, another doesn't. There isn't anything wrong with that."

Pat was crestfallen. She hadn't expected Dad to side with Gary. After all, Dad had played in the National League for four years before he accepted the Lord and later went to the mission field. She couldn't understand where his loyalty was.

As soon as they were settled in the house the mission had rented for them, Patti was going to talk to her mother about it. She had to get someone on her side.

* * *

A week later, Del and Doug Davis drove out to the airport on an errand for Danny Orlis. The boys and their sister, DeeDee, had lived with Danny and Kay since their own parents were drowned on the mission field in Guatemala. The Davis triplets were juniors at Northwest High.

"How about it, Doug?" Del began, pulling out on the highway in the direction of the airport. "Have you got a date with Tina tonight?"

"Yes, but I don't know what we're going to do. We might just go down to the Hitching Post for a sandwich."

"How about going with Letitia and me? There's

a youth rally that she wants to go to at Community Church on the south side."

"Sounds okay to me. I'll give Tina a buzz when we get home."

They were still discussing what they would do that evening when they pulled into the airport and stopped not far from the Cessna 180 that Danny used as a trainer for his advanced students. Del saw somebody behind the controls.

"Hey, look in there!" He jumped out of the car and ran quickly to the aircraft, jerking open the cabin door. "What're you doing?"

The boy was several years younger than they were. Still, he was almost as tall and broad-shouldered as they were, with blond hair and a quick, winning smile.

"Hi."

"You shouldn't be in that aircraft."

The boy swung his feet from behind the controls and jumped lightly to the ground. "You guys must be Del and Doug Davis."

"That's right," Doug retorted sternly, "but who are you, and what're you doing in the mission plane?"

"I'm Gary Trumbo."

The name didn't mean anything to either Del or Doug.

"And my dad's taking lessons in this plane. He started yesterday."

The Davis boys relaxed a little, but they were still disturbed. One thing Danny didn't tolerate was having unauthorized persons in the aircraft.

"Wasn't the plane locked?" Del persisted.

"Dad got the key from Danny. He forgot his log book yesterday." Gary was genuinely concerned at having been sitting in the airplane when they drove up. "I hope I didn't do something I wasn't supposed to. Dad said it would be all right if I sat in the plane for a minute, as long as I didn't move the controls or anything."

"In that case, I guess it was all right, but I wouldn't get in the planes without permission, if I were you."

A wistful longing crept into the boy's face. "I sure wish I could take flying lessons."

Del and Doug went into the hangar for the tools Danny wanted. Gary followed them.

"Is Danny Orlis coming out here today?" he asked.

He seemed disappointed when he learned that Danny would not be at the airport that particular Saturday.

"You could go home with us and meet him, if you want to."

Gary's frown deepened. "I guess I can wait. I just wanted to talk to him about flying. I thought maybe there was something I could do to start learning about aircraft now. Maybe there are some books I could read, or something."

"Danny could give you the names of some books on navigation and aerodynamics and weather," Del said. "But if I were you, I'd join one of the clubs for model plane builders. There are quite a few of them, and they usually go into the fundamentals of flying."

Gary had never thought of anything like that. He had put some model plane kits together, but they were the kind to hang in his room. He had never considered building a model that would actually fly.

"Do you think that would help me?" he asked, curious.

"Sure, you'd learn a lot of stuff about planes. I thought about doing it myself, but I finally decided I didn't have time."

Doug grinned. "Was that before or after you flipped over Letitia Warren?"

Del's face crimsoned.

"Cool it, old buddy."

The more Gary thought about building model planes, the more excited he became. He questioned Del and Doug as long as he could; and, when he got back home, he started calling around until he learned the name of the club leader in his neighborhood.

He talked about it with Tom Springer, a guy about his own age, who lived across the street from him. He thought perhaps Tom would go with him.

"Nothing doing," the other boy said. "Why do you want to waste your time with those guys? That wouldn't be any fun."

"It looks like fun to me."

"You can have it. I've got better things to do."

"Like what?"

"Knockin' around with the guys." He grinned mysteriously.

"Doing what?"

"I'll clue you in sometime." He glanced both directions to see if they were being watched. "Want a cigarette?"

"Those things? You've got to be kiddin'! I don't want to die of lung cancer before I'm old enough to drive a car."

Tom laughed and swaggered away.

In spite of the fact that Gary was younger than most of the guys in the model airplane club, he was invited to the next meeting.

❊   ❊   ❊

That evening after the rally, Del and Doug took their dates to the Hitching Post for something to eat. They were sitting in one of the booths near the back when Chuck Grover and his date came in. Chuck's mouth twisted into a sneer as his gaze met Del's.

"Hi."

"You're living dangerously, aren't you?" He paused briefly beside them. "I didn't think you came to wicked places like this anymore."

"Hi, Elsie," Letitia said to the girl with Chuck. Elsie ignored them. "Please, Chuck." She grasped his arm and tugged at him. "Let's go and sit down."

"Okay. Okay." He swaggered off.

When they were gone, Tina turned to Doug. "What was that all about?"

"We've had our problems with Chuck," he said. "About a year ago he gave DeeDee a bad time, and we had to lower the boom on him. I guess he never got over it."

"I can't see why a pretty gal like Elsie Powell would want to go with a character like him," Del put in.

Letitia studied the menu. "She looked as though she was about to cry. I got the impression that they had been fighting."

"If she keeps going with that guy, she'll be crying sooner or later. He's bad medicine."

"And she's crazy about him," Tina observed. "I had lunch with her the other day. He was all she could talk about."

❉   ❉   ❉

Once Gary decided to join the model plane club, he could scarcely wait for the weekly meeting night. The club leader, Harold Gibson, was particularly friendly. He met Gary at the front door and took him down the basement where the others were already hard at work.

"I'm sorry you didn't get started when the rest of the boys began work on their models, but I'll assign one of the older guys to help you catch up."

"That's great," Gary exclaimed. "I'll work extra hard." He promised himself that he wasn't going to be behind for very long. He always had been good with his hands. He'd put in enough time on his model to catch up with the others. That wasn't going to be a problem.

Mr. Gibson called Chuck Grover over and introduced him to Gary. "Chuck's been working with models longer than anyone else. He can give you the boost you need. Okay, Chuck?"

"Sure. I'll do all I can."

He was no taller than Gary but was about Del and Doug's age. Gary was going to ask if he knew them, but Chuck took him over to the bench where he was working and showed him his model. From then on, both he and Chuck were interested only in model planes.

"Just tell me what to buy so I can get started,"

Gary said, "I want to catch up with the rest of you guys as quick as I can."

"You'd better. We're all entering a contest in April. You won't be able to be in it if you don't have your model finished."

Gary was determined to get his model built in time to enter the contest, no matter what happened!

2

Gary's Disappointment

GARY TRUMBO bought the wood for his model plane and set to work building the fuselage, under Chuck Grover's direction. He did have a certain aptitude for working with his hands. It took all his skill to cut the fragile balsa wood and shape the body and wings. Because of the contest, he worked hard at it.

"Dad, they're going to have a model plane contest, and I can enter if I want to."

"Model planes?" Pat wrinkled her nose distastefully. "You mean you'd rather fool around with model planes than play football?" She couldn't understand it.

"I wasn't talking to you."

"But little kids put models together."

"Not this kind."

"They get all kinds of them. I see them at the dime store every time I go in."

"Well, you don't see this kind in the dime store," he retorted. "We make our own—except for the

motor and the radio controls. And there are high
school guys and even men working on them, so you
don't need to think you're so smart."

"I still don't know why you would want to fool
around that way when you could really be doing
something like playing football."

Ignoring her deliberately, Gary turned to his
dad. "What do you think about it?"

"It sounds great, but isn't it going to be a little
rough for you to enter against guys who are quite
a lot older and more experienced than you are?
This is your first model, you know."

"Yeah, but one of the older guys promised to
help me. He's in high school and has built four or
five planes. He knows almost as much about it as
Mr. Gibson does. He says that all I have to do is
order an engine and radio controls and I'll be all
set."

At that, his dad hesitated. "Money's a little tight
around our place right now, Gary. How expensive
are they going to be?"

The boy's excitement dimmed. "That's what I
wanted to talk to you about. A good one is real expensive, but they last for a long time."

"That's not the point. It sounds to me as though
they may cost a lot more than we'll be able to afford. You've got to remember that I'm still a missionary and that we've got to live on a missionary's
allowance while I'm in flight school."

"I've got to have them, or there's no use in even building the plane."

Virgil Trumbo was slow in answering. He pulled in a deep breath and sighed. "I'm sorry, Gary, but I don't think you'd better count on getting either the model engine or the radio controls."

The boy stared at him incredulously. He must not have understood his dad correctly. There had to be some mistake.

"But Dad!"

"Unless you can earn the money yourself, you can't get them."

Gary said no more about it. His dad had made up his mind, and there was no use arguing with him. He realized that was the end of it.

Pat followed him into the other room after they finished eating. "I'm sorry, Gary," she told him.

"I'll bet you are!"

"Honest I am. And I'm going to pray that you'll get those things you need, even if you don't play football."

"There's no use in doing that." Self-pity seized him. "I've already decided I'm going to quit working on it."

She fought back sudden tears.

He was sorry he had spoken to her so harshly, but there was no use in kidding himself, or her, either. Without a motor and radio controls, there was no use going on. He had just as well quit and save himself all that work.

Most of the time he was glad he was a missionary's son, but right now he sure wasn't. If his dad had a job like ordinary fathers, he wouldn't have to drop out of the contest. There would be money enough to buy what he needed.

When club meeting night came around, he changed his mind about not going. He had to tell Chuck and Mr. Gibson that he was quitting. He couldn't have them think he was mad, and he had to pick up his model and the material he had already bought. There was no need to throw it away. He just might be able to finish it sometime.

He was a little late when he got there. Mr. Gibson was busy with a couple of other guys, so Gary went over and talked to Chuck.

"You mean you really have to quit?" The older boy sounded genuinely disappointed.

Gary's lower lip trembled. "There's no use doing anything else. Dad says there isn't any money for an engine and the radio controls I'd have to have."

"They don't cost all that much."

For the first time Gary began to explain for his dad, making excuses for him for not being able to buy the controls and engine. "Dad's only a missionary," he went on lamely, "and we're living on a missionary's allowance while he's taking flight instruction."

Interest flecked Chuck's eyes. "You mean he's a *pilot?*"

"That's right. He's here getting some advanced flight instruction from Danny Orlis."

For a time, Chuck was silent. A strange look that somehow disturbed Gary, twisted his face.

"Orlis?" the older boy echoed. "Is that the guy the Davis triplets live with?"

"Yeah, do you know them?"

He hesitated once more. "I know their sister better. Are Del and Doug good friends of yours?"

"I'll say they are. Next to you, Chuck, they're just about the best friends I've got in Rock Point."

Chuck Grover straightened slowly, a smile spreading across his face and replacing the sneer. So, Gary was one of those religious people, too.

"Don't be so shook up about not having a motor and controls. I think maybe I can help you."

At first Gary was sure that he hadn't heard Chuck correctly. "You don't mean that," he said. Chuck had to be joking or just trying to get his hopes built up. "You're just kidding me."

"No, I'm not. I'm giving it to you straight. If you're a good friend of Doug and Del's, I'll sure see that you get all the help you need."

"Man, that's great!"

Chuck turned to face Gary directly and leaned against the bench. His voice was guarded. "There's one thing you've got to promise me first."

He might have known there would be a condition to it.

"What's that?" he asked suspiciously.

"I don't want them or anyone else to know anything about it. Okay?"

Gary couldn't see the reason for that. "Why not?"

"I just don't want anyone to know that I'm helping you, that's all. If you'll promise me that, I'll see that you get the engine and radio controls you need."

The younger boy hesitated.

"If you don't give me your word you won't say anything to anyone, everything's off. You'd just as well get your model and go home."

"You can count on me. I won't say a word."

"Not to anybody?"

"Not to anybody."

"Okay. I believe you. Now, let's go to work on that model of yours. Who knows? You just might beat us all."

Gary laughed excitedly. Chuck was just about the best friend a guy could ever have. He didn't even think Del or Doug would do anything like that for him.

When Gary got home that night, Pat was waiting for him. She saw the bounce in his step and knew something had happened.

"You didn't quit, did you?"

"Nope." He couldn't lie to her. Besides, he didn't even want to.

"What happened?"

He paused uneasily. He couldn't tell her that Chuck was getting the items he needed. He'd given his word that he wouldn't. But he had to tell her something.

"I decided to finish the model," he answered, hoping that would satisfy her. It did.

"And you're going to trust God to get you the motor and—and that other thing you need."

He remained silent.

"And you were the one who said it wouldn't do any good to pray! You just wait! You're going to get those things before the contest. I'm going to pray and pray and pray until you do."

His smile flashed. "Thanks, Pat." She was a good kid, he decided, even if she was a brat.

*   *   *

Gary saw Tom Springer several times in the next few weeks and tried to interest him in joining the club, but without success.

"I told you I don't have time for that stuff. How about you joining my club? We'll show you some real excitement. Come with us a couple of times, and those model plane club meetings will be so dull you won't want to fool with them, either."

Gary knew he wouldn't be interested in getting in with Tom and his friends. He had been hearing about them ever since he moved to Rock Point with his folks. He was sure they did a lot of bragging about things they had never done, but some of it had to be true. A newspaper article would refer to vandalism or breaking into a small shop or some old person's home, and Tom and his buddies would swagger about school hinting that they were responsible.

At family devotions, Gary mentioned Tom often, asking the others to pray for him.

"Have you tried talking to him about Jesus Christ?" his dad asked.

The boy hesitated. How did a guy go about sharing Christ with a character like Tom? Say anything, and he'd be the laughing stock of the school.

"I—I think I'd better get more acquainted with him first," he rationalized.

*　*　*

Gary continued to work on his model plane every chance he got. He came directly home from school every afternoon, finished his homework, and went to the basement. There in his dad's workshop he cut out the framework of his small plane, glued it together, and covered it with tough, lightweight paper. And whenever he had a problem, he asked Chuck about it when their club met. He spent so much time working on his model that he soon caught up with the others, in spite of the fact that he got a late start.

At last he was ready for the engine and radio controls that Chuck Grover had promised to loan him. He asked his friend about them once or twice, but got no definite answer. The older boy passed it off casually.

"I'll get them for you one of these days. You won't need them before the contest, anyway."

"We'll have to mount the engine and check it out," Gary reminded him uneasily.

For some reason, Chuck didn't act nearly as sure of his ability to get the engine and radio control as he had previously.

"All I've got to do is to see this guy I loaned them to and have him give them back to me. You'll get them in plenty of time."

Gary waited hopefully. Chuck had acted so irritated when he talked with him about them, he didn't feel that he should say anything more. For the first time the boy began to doubt that he would get the equipment he needed. It didn't look as though Chuck was going to be able to deliver. And he knew there wasn't any use in his trying to get them himself. He didn't even have a job.

If he didn't get the engine and radio controls, the model plane would be useless as far as the contest was concerned. The competition was to be judged mostly on performance. That meant he would have to have both items, or he wouldn't be able to enter.

As the days passed, he was so depressed that his folks noticed and asked about it.

"Is there something wrong at school?" his dad asked.

"Oh no," he said quickly. "Everything's fine."

"Are your grades up?"

"As far as I know. I haven't had any failing marks, even on my daily papers."

Only Patti eyed him knowingly, and she didn't say anything. He was grateful for that. As she passed him on the way to her room, she whispered that she was still praying for him.

At last, two weeks before the contest, Gary went to Chuck once more.

"I hate to bring it up again, but we'll have to get with it about those controls and the engine if we're going to get them installed and checked out."

Chuck squinted uncomfortably at him. "I've been meaning to talk with you about those parts, Gary."

The boy caught his concern. "You mean you're not going to be able to get them for me?"

Chuck had a difficult time answering. "I didn't know it, but the guy I loaned them to wrecked the plane—slammed her into a rock. He split the engine right in two!"

Gary gasped. The engine was wrecked! Now he wouldn't be able to enter the contest after all!

3

Chuck Comes Through

IT WAS A FULL MINUTE before Gary Trumbo could force himself to speak. It had happened just as he feared it would. He wasn't going to get to enter the model plane contest after all. He had spent months working on his plane, and now he wasn't even going to get to see if it would fly!

"What about the radio controls?" he asked numbly. Not that it mattered any. Without an engine, the radio controls wouldn't do him any good.

"They went on the fritz," Chuck explained. "That was the reason the plane crashed."

Gary turned away to mask his disappointment. He should have known it was too much for him to expect that Chuck would loan him the expensive parts he needed. People just didn't do things like that.

"I'm real sorry about it," Chuck said, putting aside the screwdriver he had been using. "I'd do most anything I could to make it up to you." He shrugged. "But I don't know what to do."

Gary managed a weak smile. At first he had wondered if Chuck had been playing a game with him all along and had never intended to get the parts for him, but now he could doubt it no longer. He had to be sincere about it.

"That's okay. You couldn't help it."

"Don't get so shook up," Chuck told him. "Maybe you'll get to enter the contest after all."

"That's a laugh!"

"I'm not making any promises, but hang in there. You might get to enter that contest yet."

Gary could not understand it. Chuck did a lot of kidding around, and half the time Gary couldn't tell whether he meant what he was saying or not, but this time he sounded serious—as serious as he had before when he had first promised Gary the parts.

"But how am I going to do it?" the younger boy wanted to know. "I don't have any money, and the way it looks, there's not much chance that I'm going to have any. At least not enough to make a dent in what those things cost."

"Did I say you had to have money?" Chuck retorted, contempt honing his voice. "I'm not making any promises, but I think I've got an idea for getting something for you. And if I do, it'll be a lot better than the junk I was going to let you use, believe me."

Three nights later, Chuck Grover drove by the junior high building just as classes were dismissed. He called Gary over to the car.

"Hi. Hop in. I'll give you a lift home."

Gary did so.

"Going to club tonight?" Chuck wanted to know.

"I don't think so. It wouldn't do any good now. I won't have an entry in the contest, and that's all everyone else will be talking about."

"The trouble with you is, you don't think positively. I'm surprised at you."

"I know what it was like last week. And every time I turned around, somebody was asking me what I was going to be doing with my plane or if I'd flown her yet." He shook his head. "Nope, there's no use in my going to the meeting tonight."

"You can suit yourself," Chuck told him, "but if you want to get your plane ready to fly, you'd better be there."

"I'm afraid my rubber band motor wouldn't get me very far in the competition." He didn't intend to be sarcastic, but there was an edge on his voice.

"Turn around and look on the seat behind you," Chuck said, laughing.

Gary did as he was told.

"Now, answer me. Does that look like a rubber band engine?"

"Man, oh, man! Where did you get that?"

Silence.

"Where'd you get 'em, man?"

"I had some stuff a buddy of mine wanted, so I traded him for them."

Gary picked up the boxes that were lying on the back seat and opened them. He whistled his amazement. "They're the best there is!"

Chuck's grin widened. "That's the way I do things. First class all the way."

Gary's excitement melted. Those things weren't for him. They were far too good for Chuck or anyone else to loan to him—especially when Chuck was having an entry in the contest himself. This was more of Chuck's teasing. He planned on using them himself.

"You ought to do all right Saturday," Gary grumbled.

"What do you mean, *I* ought to do all right?"

"You wouldn't loan me stuff like this."

"Why not? You're my friend." Chuck kept his eyes on the road.

The boy studied the engine and the radio controls, his awe increasing. "Do you really mean it? You're going to let me use them?"

"I said I'd get you what you needed, didn't I?"

Gary opened the box and removed the engine. It was still in its original wrapping. "You won't have anything half this good yourself."

The older boy shrugged. "I've entered the contest for the last three years. It's time I helped someone else."

Gary still could scarcely believe this was happening to him. "And you're letting me use them?"

"On one condition. I still don't want you to tell anybody where you got them. Okay?"

Gary Trumbo turned back to the plane engine and the remote control unit, examining them carefully.

"This must've cost a lot of bread, man!"

"Like I said," Chuck explained indifferently, "I traded a buddy out of them. He wanted an old pair of skis and a couple of poles I had, and I knew you needed the engine and the radio controls, so we made a deal."

Gary studied the radio. The price was still on the box. "They must have been *some* skis if he made a trade for these."

Chuck squirmed uncomfortably. "As a matter of fact, the guy bought this stuff to use himself. Then he decided that making model planes wasn't for him. I think he'd have traded for anything just to get rid of them."

"I've done a lot of looking around, trying to find something I could afford. These are the best there is." He glanced up at his companion. "Why don't you put them on your plane, Chuck, and let me use your old ones?"

"Oh, no." He spoke quickly. "My plane's all set and balanced. I wouldn't go through all of that again."

"But this stuff is so much better than what you have."

The older boy's eyes narrowed. "What're you kicking about? I'm satisfied. And you ought to be. These parts aren't costing you a cent."

"And you really want me to have them?"

"That's why I traded for them," Chuck told him, an injured tone creeping into his voice. "But if you don't want them, forget it. I can always find someone to take them off my hands."

"Sure, I want them," Gary retorted quickly. Now that the items were his, he wasn't going to do anything to lose them, that was sure. "I don't know how I can ever thank you."

"And you're not going to say anything to anyone about where you got them. Remember, that's part of the deal. If you tell anyone—anyone at all— I want them back."

The younger boy was quick to reply. "I won't say a word to anyone—except my folks, that is."

The driver's eyes darkened, and he glanced quickly at the boy beside him. "I said I don't want you to tell anyone. That includes your folks. Understand?"

"But they won't say anything to anyone. I can guarantee it. They know how to keep a secret."

Chuck shook his head angrily. "Oh, no. If that's the way things are, my offer is off. Just forget I ever showed 'em to you."

A vast, chilling emptiness swept over Gary. "You mean you're not going to let me have them after all?"

"Not if you're going to tell your old man."

"But—"

"I thought I could trust you."

"You can." His mouth had the taste of wet cotton. "I won't say anything to anyone about where I got them."

Chuck Grover still hesitated. "Not even your folks?" he repeated.

Gary had never kept anything from his dad before. He had always told him what he was doing and who he was with, but he had never faced a situation quite like this one. He didn't know why Chuck was so anxious to have him keep quiet, but he must have his reasons. And he couldn't see how it could hurt to keep this from his folks. It was something like somebody giving money to the church, he decided, and not wanting anyone to know about it.

"It may sound stupid to you," Chuck continued, "but there are a lot of guys in the club who think you're not going to get anywhere with your model because you're not as old or as experienced as they are. I don't want you to say anything to anyone because I want to see you sandbag those characters."

Gary wasn't quite sure he followed Chuck's reasoning. "Why would that make any difference to you?"

"Because I've been helping you, stupid! And I want those guys to know that you're not quite as dumb as they think you are. But if you don't want to win the contest, just forget the whole thing. I'm sorry I wasted my time on you."

"Okay." He spoke reluctantly. "I won't say anything to anyone, not even my dad."

The older boy was relieved. "You're sure of that?"

"Positive."

"That's better. I know I can trust you."

The following night after school, Chuck Grover picked up Gary again, and they went over to his house, where they used his garage workshop to make the installation. Gary watched admiringly as Chuck mounted the engine. It was easy to see that Chuck had put a number of motors and remote control units in the planes he had built over the last three years. He knew exactly how to go about it.

*   *   *

Letitia Warren had been increasingly concerned about Elsie Powell since their encounter at the Hitching Post.

"Have you noticed her lately, DeeDee?" she asked Del's sister as they were having lunch together. "She looks miserable."

"Who wouldn't? She's dating Chuck. He wouldn't be happy unless he was giving her a bad time."

Letitia was silent. She had been outspoken in her faith since the day a few months before when she came back to Christ, but she had never once thought about sharing her faith in Christ with Elsie. The vivacious little redhead seemed so sparkling and full of fun that Letitia hadn't realized that she, too, needed Jesus.

"We should be praying for her."

DeeDee agreed.

In the next few days, Letitia tried hard to make friends with Elsie. The other girl seemed to respond, but only until Letitia mentioned Jesus Christ.

"Religion can't do anything to solve my problems." The tears were close.

"That's what I used to think. Then I learned that Jesus Christ is the answer to all of my problems. He wants to be in every hour of every day of our lives, guiding and helping us."

Elsie didn't understand. "The only one who can help me is Chuck Grover." For some reason she felt she could confide in Letitia. "If he would just quit going with other girls, I wouldn't have any problems. He knows how it makes me feel, and he keeps on doing it anyway."

Letitia had never gone steady or become so uptight over anyone, but she thought she knew how Elsie felt.

"I'll be praying for you," she said softly.

"I've got to run," the other girl said, but her eyes thanked Letitia wordlessly.

4

Elsie's Problem

GARY HADN'T REALIZED that his promise to Chuck could cause him trouble, but it did. He had been taking his model home with him from time to time so his dad could see the progress he was making on it. Now, with the engine in it and the radio control unit hooked up, he could not let anyone in the family see it. If he did, they would be sure to ask questions. He wasn't going to lie to them—and especially not to his dad. That was something he had never done.

The only answer was for him to keep the plane away from the house and hope his folks didn't ask too many questions about it. When he got home for dinner the evening he and Chuck finished mounting the engine, his dad asked where he had been.

He paused on the way to his room but did not turn around. "Working on my plane."

"How's it coming?"

"Okay."

"I still wish I could have bought you the engine and the controls you need for it, but it's out of the question. We just don't have the money to spend on that sort of thing."

The boy's cheeks darkened. He couldn't understand why it upset him so much to talk to his dad about the plane. He hadn't done anything he shouldn't. He wasn't keeping quiet about the things Chuck gave him because he was trying to deceive his folks or wanted to keep something from them. It was only because Chuck insisted on it.

And what else could he do? His friend was asking little enough of him when he insisted that he keep quiet about where he got them. Gary didn't like the idea of keeping things from his parents, but he sure wasn't going to break his word after what Chuck had done for him.

As soon as he could get away from his dad, he went into the bedroom and closed the door. It would be easier to stay in there for a little while than to answer his questions.

The following afternoon as soon as school was out for the day, Chuck took him out to an open field to test the plane. He started the engine and launched the model breathlessly. That was the time when it could crack up and ruin months of work.

But it flew very well, responding to the controls as smoothly as a manned aircraft.

"Look at her, Chuck!" Admiration crept into his voice. "Just look at her! Did you ever see anything so beautiful?"

"I told you she'd fly like a bird."

"It's that engine you loaned me," Gary answered.

"I wouldn't say that. You did a good job of building your model, or the best engine in the world wouldn't make her fly the way she does."

Working the controls, Gary let the plane circle for a minute and describe two figure eights before he brought the plane back to the road, landing her a dozen yards away from the place where they were standing.

"I'm going to make a prediction right now," Chuck said, exultant. "You're going to win one of the prizes. I wouldn't be surprised if you got first."

"Do you really think so?"

"I don't see how you can miss." His grin widened. "Then won't everybody be surprised!"

They got in the car and started back to town.

"There's only one thing that bothers me right now," Gary observed. "My folks are going to know that I'm in the contest. When they find out, Dad's going to ask plenty of questions about the engine and radio controls. He's going to want to know where I got them and why you gave them to me."

Chuck squinted darkly at him. For an instant,

apprehension lurked in the shadows of his mind.

"You aren't forgetting what you promised me, are you?"

"That's what's bothering me."

"Well, don't forget. You promised to keep your mouth shut about where you got them."

"I know that." In spite of himself, desperation crept in. "But what am I going to tell them?"

Chuck Grover shrugged his indifference. "That's your problem. Tell them anything you want to. The only thing I can say is, you'd better keep shut about where you got them, or I'll be off you for life."

"Don't worry." He spoke defensively. "I told you I wasn't going to tell them where I got the stuff, and I'm not going to."

"See that you don't."

The contest was to begin the following Saturday morning, with the finals that afternoon. Gary tried hard to think of something he could tell his folks that would protect his word to Chuck and still avoid lying, but he could come up with nothing.

The only thing he could do, he decided, was not to enter the contest at all. Chuck might not like that. He didn't like the idea much himself, but it seemed to be the only solution to his problem.

Then his folks decided to go away to a missionary conference for the weekend. They wanted him to go, too, but he begged them to let him stay with Danny and Kay.

"I want to be here for the model plane contest, Dad," he said. "I've *got* to see how things come out."

"I'd forgotten all about that," his dad said.

"Then you mean I can stay?"

"Well," Virgil answered thoughtfully, "I can see why you'd want to be here for it."

"Can I stay, too?" Pat asked.

"Why do you want to stay?" Gary asked. If she stayed home, he'd still be in trouble. She'd tell the folks as soon as they got back.

"I want to see if you win."

"I'm afraid Gary's not going to be able to enter his model in the contest, Pat," their dad said. "He doesn't have a motor or the remote control unit. Besides, I think you had better go with us."

Surprisingly, she didn't object. Instead, she faced her brother almost accusingly. "If you'd gone out for football instead of fooling around with that kid stuff, you wouldn't have all those problems."

"Lay off, will you?"

She stuck the tip of her tongue out at him before flouncing into the other room. When she was gone, Gary asked his dad again if he could stay home that weekend. He still hadn't had an answer.

"If it's all right with Mother and Danny and Kay, it's all right with me."

Gary tried to mask his relief. He would be able to enter the contest and not have to lie to his folks either. He was so happy, his mother noticed and mentioned it.

"You act as though you're glad we're going to be gone for the weekend."

The boy flushed. "I just want to be at the contest, that's all."

* * *

Tom Springer heard about the Trumbos' leaving for the weekend and talked with Gary about it.

"So your folks are going away and leaving you at home. Are you ever lucky!"

His eyes narrowed. "What do you mean?"

"You can do anything you want to for a whole weekend. Man, I think I'll get the guys and come over to visit you."

"I'm not going to be at home. I'm staying with—" He was about to tell Tom he would be at the Orlis home, but decided against it. Tom knew Danny by reputation. If he found out that Gary was staying there, he'd get on his back about religion. "I'm staying with friends."

"That's tough. Maybe we'll have to go over and visit you anyway—even if you aren't at home."

Gary knew what he was referring to. Another neighbor had gone somewhere; and, when they came back, they discovered that someone had broken in and had a party in the basement. Tom had never said for sure, but Gary had the idea he and his pals were responsible.

"You wouldn't!"

Tom paused, as though trying to make up his mind. "Nope," he said at last. "I guess I wouldn't. You're a friend of mine."

* * *

Letitia continued to pray for Elsie Powell, although she did not have a chance to share her faith with her again in the next several weeks. That was the situation when she met Elsie in the library. Letitia had a book to check out for an English Literature assignment and went back to the shelves to get it. There, at a back table, Elsie was sitting with her head buried in her arms.

"Elsie," Letitia said softly, putting a hand on the other girl's trembling shoulder. "What's wrong?"

No answer.

"What is it, Elsie?"

"Leave me alone!" She looked up, eyes blazing. And then she saw it was Letitia. "Oh, it's you. I'm sorry. I thought it was someone else, and there aren't many people I—I even want to talk to right now."

The Warren girl sat down beside her and spoke in a whisper. "Can I help you?"

"We can't talk here. Miss Turner will be back on our necks any minute."

"We can go out and sit in Hank's car. He's out for baseball, so he won't need it till after six."

Letitia got the book she wanted, and she and Elsie went out to her brother's car in the parking lot. By the time they got there, most of the other cars were gone, leaving them virtually alone. Neither of them said anything until they were in the front seat and had shut the doors.

"Is there something you'd like to tell me?"

Elsie shrugged. "I don't know why I'm even wasting your time," she said miserably. "There isn't anything you can do. There's nothing anybody can do—now." She went on to tell Letitia that she and Chuck had broken up. "I couldn't stand it anymore," she went on. "But I really didn't want to break up with him. I just got tired of his not showing up for dates and making fun of me when I felt bad because he was going with other girls. I was only trying to talk to him about it, but he laughed at me and said we'd just as well cut it off, that he was tired of me anyway."

She started to cry again. When her sobbing began to ease, she continued her story.

"Right now I'm just about as low as I can get. I keep thinking there's no use in trying to go on," she said brokenly.

"I've never been through anything quite like what you're going through," the Warren girl said, "but I do know what it's like. I used to feel miserable most of the time."

Elsie looked at Letitia as though she could not possibly understand unless she herself had been jilted by a boyfriend.

"Right now I feel as though I'd like to go to the top of Pike's Peak and jump off," she said aloud. "Life isn't worth living!"

Letitia nodded to show that she understood. "There was a time when I didn't have any friends—not even any girl friends—and the boys *never* asked me for a date. I used to feel so sorry for myself I could hardly stand it. I was miserable."

The other girl's lips quivered, and her temper got away from her. "I don't feel sorry for myself. I'm just facing reality! Nobody cares about me! There isn't any use in living anymore!"

5

The Contest

BRIEFLY LETITIA PRAYED for guidance. It was so
hard to know what to say to someone who was as
upset as her companion was.

Elsie fought to maintain control of herself. And
when she spoke, her voice trembled. "You can say
what you want, but you'll never make me believe
that anybody cares about me. If something did
happen to me, it wouldn't make any difference to
anyone in Rock Point—except maybe my folks, and
I'm not even sure it would matter to them."

Letitia quietly protested that her friend was
wrong. Here she was on sure ground. She had experienced the same doubt and bewilderment, the
same frustration and feelings of inferiority and self-
pity.

"That's not true, Elsie," she answered. "Even if
you were right about the people in Rock Point—
which you're not—you still aren't alone. The Lord
Jesus understands and cares. He cares about each

of us." She went on to tell her friend about her own despair, repeating much of what she had said a few moments before.

Elsie knew some of the story. Most of the kids in Northwest knew how miserable Letitia had been before the skiing accident in which she broke her back, and how radiant she became when she finally turned to Jesus Christ. But she had never heard Letitia tell about it and how she felt.

She listened intently as the other girl explained how Christ had worked in her life, taking her out of her self-pity and bringing her to Himself. "He didn't take away my trouble, as I asked Him to. He did something better than that for me. He gave me the courage I needed to face my problems. He became my strength and gave me victory over everything that had happened to me, making me happy in spite of the difficulties."

"You can't be serious," the other girl said at last. "Religion is all right for church and Sunday school and—and for people who are about to die, but it doesn't help you to *live!*"

"Jesus Christ does!" Letitia spoke so confidently the other girl listened intently. "He has helped me to be happy regardless of the circumstances."

She went on to relate that there were problems at home that bothered her a great deal at times. Her dad still had periods of depression when he felt that everyone was against him and that he would never be able to get a job he liked that would pay enough for the family to live on comfortably. Her mother got upset, too, and Letitia had to confess there were times when she didn't trust God the way she should and was disturbed because things hadn't changed fast enough to suit her.

"I used to get so uptight I didn't think I could stand it," she concluded. "But God has helped me. He has given me victory over those times. I used to be an added burden to my folks when they had trouble. Now I think I'm able to help them."

Elsie wasn't ready to accept all of that. "It sounds nice, but I never could be that way. There's no use in even trying."

"God knows how weak we are, Elsie. That's why He gives us a new life. All we have to do is put our trust in Him, and He will give us the strength we need to face whatever comes."

Before Hank returned to his car an hour later, Letitia had prayed with Elsie. The distraught girl gave her heart to Jesus Christ.

Letitia was so excited that night, she could hardly sleep. When she came to the Lord it seemed as though that was the biggest event in her life. Up until that time, she had never been able to share Christ effectively with anyone.

She used to say she was witnessing when she asked someone to go to Sunday school or church, and would ask people to pray that God would help her to witness to more people. She had been so proud of anything she had done. Now she saw what it was really like to share Jesus Christ with someone else who had a need.

And Elsie had responded. Her heart soared! The words of the song, "How Great Thou Art" kept going through her mind.

Although she had not slept more than a few hours, she got up early the next morning, she was so excited. She hurried to school and waited near DeeDee's locker for her friend to come in. She *had* to tell her about Elsie. She had only been waiting for a minute or so when Chuck Grover stopped to talk to her. The instant he did so, she realized that Elsie had told him she was now a Christian.

"Got any good sermons for me this morning, Letitia?" he asked, a sneer in his voice.

She acted as though she had not felt the cutting edge of his tone. "I can tell you that Jesus Christ gave me a new life," she said. "And I can tell you that I'm happier since I came to Him than I've ever been before."

If he was impressed, he did a good job of hiding it from her.

"My, my, isn't that tremendous?"

"And He can do the same for you, if you'll let Him."

He laughed raucously. The kids at the far end

of the hall turned quickly to look at them. Letitia's cheeks were crimson.

"I understand you got to Elsie. Congratulations. I thought she was too smart to buy that garbage."

"Elsie saw the claims that Jesus Christ has on her life and realized that to be happy she had to confess her sin and put her trust in Him. You can have that same peace too, Chuck, if you'll only do what she did."

"Hah! You'd just as well save your breath," he sneered. "I'm not buying any today. But I'll tell you what, Letitia. You did me a favor taking that stupid Elsie off my back. She doesn't want to have anything to do with me now. And that's a relief. She's been hounding me ever since I decided she isn't the gal for me. Now I'm going to give you all my religion business. I was going to give it to Dee-Dee, but I don't think she'd appreciate it. If I ever decide that I'm tired of the old Chuck Grover and want a new one, you'll be the first to know. Okay?"

Tears came to her eyes, and she fought them. Since praying with Elsie the afternoon before, Jesus Christ was so close to her she thought everyone else would feel that same reverence. It hurt to hear Chuck make light of her Lord.

"I might even come and let you pray with me," he continued. "How about that? That ought to make you real happy."

She wanted to protest, but there was nothing she

could say. He wasn't serious. He wanted only to ridicule her faith. Realizing that hurt so much she could no longer keep back the tears. It seemed to please him when he saw that he made her cry.

"You don't have to bawl about it. I thought you'd be glad." He knew he was scoring, and he kept at it fiendishly. "That's what you want, isn't it? What do you get if you win me as a convert? Will it put a star in your crown?"

"Please, Chuck."

"I'm just trying to get things lined up good for you. You ought to get two stars for getting hold of a guy like me." He raised his voice so the kids going by could hear him. "Maybe if I hold out a little, you'll get an extra one. Is that the way it works?"

He was still laughing boisterously as he went down the hall and turned in to the library. Letitia still had not moved when DeeDee came up. The Davis girl saw immediately that something was wrong, and asked about it.

"There's nothing wrong with me." She wiped the tears away. "It's Chuck Grover."

"You've been talking to him?" she asked. She knew already what Letitia meant.

"I tried to talk to him. All he did was make fun of me."

"I know all about him."

"You didn't hear it, too, did you?"

"Not just now, but I've been through it with

him. I know just about what he said and did. I got the same sort of treatment."

Letitia hesitated. Her first reaction was to get so mad she wouldn't even pray for Chuck. That, she realized, wasn't the right attitude.

"We'll just have to pray all the more for him," she said.

*   *   *

The Trumbos left that weekend for the missionary conference, and Gary stayed with Danny and Kay. When they talked as though they would like to go to the park for the model plane contest, Gary discouraged them.

"You can come if you want to," he said, "but I'm just a novice. I don't think my model will win anything."

Both statements were true, but they weren't the reason he wanted to go alone. Having them there would be almost the same as having his folks. He hadn't realized how hard it was to keep something from someone who was close to him. He had to consider everything he did and try to decide whether it would give him away or not. In that area, at least, what he had done was almost like lying. Tell one lie, and a guy had to tell sixteen others and remember every one of them in order to keep from being found out. He had to do a lot of scheming to keep his word to Chuck Grover.

"Wouldn't you like a ride over to the park?" Kay asked him.

He thanked her and told her that he would be walking over with some guys from the club.

The afternoon before the contest was one of the longest Gary ever put in. He tried to study, but the words skipped across the page and ran together. He had difficulty even keeping his mind on what the teacher was saying. He was glad they didn't have any tests that day. If he had, he would have failed them for sure.

Before he left that morning, she told him again that she was free and could drive him to the park if he wanted her to, but he told her that he would just as soon walk. That wasn't actually true. He didn't like walking any better than any other guy his age, but he didn't want her at the contest. If she came, she would see the engine and radio controls on his plane and was sure to mention them to his folks. He couldn't have her there.

As it was, he didn't have to walk out to the park. Chuck Grover picked him up and gave him a ride.

"All set to win?"

Gary licked his lips. "I'm sure going to try."

"You'll wipe 'em out in your class." He glanced at the younger boy's model. "In a way, I'm glad you're not going to be entered against me. I don't think I'd have a chance."

Gary knew Chuck was only kidding, but it

pleased him to hear his older friend talk that way.

The novice class competition was held first, and Gary was the fourth to fly his plane. He was so nervous he had a little trouble getting the engine started, but when he did, he flew his model expertly, running it through the prescribed maneuvers with the skill of a veteran. A cheer went up from the handful of spectators as he brought it in for a superb landing.

"See, what'd I tell you?"

Before Gary could reply, one of the spectators pushed his way through the crowd.

"Hello, young man."

A smile pulled at the corners of Gary's mouth as he recognized the speaker. "Hello, there, Mr. King."

"I'd like to take a look at that plane of yours."

"Oh, sure." He handed it to the man.

"Make it yourself?"

"Most of it," he answered.

The man's facial muscles tightened. "Where did you get your engine and control unit?"

Gary hesitated, the color seeping slowly from his cheeks. He couldn't say anything. He had promised Chuck he wouldn't.

"I—"

"You don't have to tell me. I checked the serial numbers. That's the pair that were stolen from my hobby store."

6

The Accusation

A GASP RIPPLED through the small crowd at the man's charge. Gary recoiled involuntarily, as though he had been hit in the face.

"You stole both the engine and the radio control unit from my store!" Mr. King repeated the charge. "I thought I'd find them if I came down here!"

"But I didn't steal them! Honest I didn't!" A desperate pleading filled the boy's young voice. He had gone into the hobby store often enough, looking at the engines and control units. He didn't suppose anyone else had made as many trips in to see them or had asked as many questions about them. He could see why Mr. King would suspect him, but he hadn't done it. He had to make him understand somehow. "I didn't steal them," he repeated. "I give you my word that I didn't!"

"It shouldn't be too difficult to prove that you're innocent. Suppose you show me the sales slips for them."

He glanced in Chuck's direction helpless. "I—I—"

"Do you have them, or don't you?"

The boy shook his head.

"That's understandable," Mr. King continued angrily. "You don't have them because you didn't buy either item. The police know that, too. I turned in the serial numbers right after the pieces turned up missing."

Gary's eyes widened, and he stared hard at Chuck. Surely the older boy was going to come forward and tell Mr. King that he hadn't stolen the engine and control unit. They were friends. He couldn't let him take the blame.

"There's something wrong. I didn't steal either of those things."

"There's something wrong, all right! You stole them from me and got caught! Now, where are your folks? I've got to talk to them."

"They—they're not home this weekend."

"A likely story. You probably sneaked off so they wouldn't know their son is a thief."

"I'm telling you the truth. They're gone. They won't be back until tomorrow night."

"That doesn't make any real difference now," the store owner said triumphantly. "I can wait and talk to them when they get back. There's plenty of time for me to bring charges against you if I don't get any satisfaction out of your dad."

Gary's face whitened.

"There's one thing you should know, young man. I've had it with kids stealing half my stock. I'm going to make an example out of you, if it's the last thing I ever do."

Gary stared miserably at him as he whirled and stalked away. For almost a minute after the hobby store owner left, a hush settled over the group of kids and their parents. At last the chief judge spoke.

"I'm sorry, son, but we'll have to disqualify your entry. Under the circumstances, we can't do anything else."

"But I—I didn't do it. I'm telling you the truth."

"For your sake, I hope you didn't. But it wouldn't be fair to the others for us to allow your entry to stand. The other guys have all lived up to the rules. They shouldn't have to compete against someone who may have shoplifted parts for his model."

They wouldn't even let Gary take his model home with him. They told him they would have to keep it until they determined whether he had stolen the parts or not.

Gary looked for Chuck to talk to him, as soon as he could get away from Mr. King, but he couldn't find him anywhere in the park. As soon as he got back to Danny and Kay's, he went to the phone and called for Chuck.

"I'm sorry," his mother said. "Charles isn't home, and I have no idea when he will be back."

"Thanks." He returned the receiver to its cradle.

Danny and Doug, who came in just then, had heard nothing about the trouble at the park.

"How'd it go for you this afternoon?" Danny asked.

"Terrible."

Danny thought the boy was referring to his own standing in the contest and was about to tease him gently, but he saw the despair in Gary's face and realized it was more than getting beat.

"You look as though something terrible did happen."

The boy did not answer him, but whirled and stormed tearfully to the spare bedroom where he was sleeping for the weekend. Doug turned to Danny.

"What's eatin' him?" he asked, curious.

"I don't know, but I'm going to find out."

Danny Orlis went to the bedroom door and knocked softly. There was no answer. After a moment he opened the door and slipped inside. The boy was sprawled on the bed, sobs shaking his thin shoulders.

"Gary," Danny said, "I think you and I ought to have a little talk. What's this all about?"

When Gary saw that Danny was not going to leave the room until he learned what was troubling him, he choked back the sobbing and sat up.

"They say I stole it, but I didn't!" His voice trembled with emotion. "I swear I didn't, Danny! I didn't take those things."

"Who says you stole what?"

Gary told him about the contest and Mr. King's accusation. "But I'm telling the truth, Danny," he repeated. "I didn't steal them!"

"Where did you get them?"

The boy hesitated. "Somebody gave them to me—I mean, a friend of mine loaned them to me."

"Who is he?"

At first Gary refused to say. "I promised I wouldn't tell," he said defensively. "That's the only way he would let me use them."

"That promise isn't binding now, Gary." Danny was gentle but firm. "A serious charge has been made against you. You're going to have to tell everything you know about the engine and radio control unit, regardless of who it hurts."

The boy was not going to tell Danny about Chuck, in spite of the difficult situation he was in. Danny, however, would not allow him to remain silent. He continued to press until he learned that it was Chuck Grover who had loaned the engine and radio controls to him.

"But you aren't going to tell anyone, are you?"

"I can't make a promise like that," Danny said firmly. "Your dad will have to know, for one."

"But I promised Chuck that I wouldn't tell any-one—particularly not my folks."

"That doesn't make any difference now. You have to tell them, if they're going to be able to help you. They've got to know everything about the arrangement."

After a few minutes, during which he talked with Gary at length about Chuck's part in the affair, Danny went to the kitchen, where Kay was preparing lunch.

"Did you find out anything?" she asked quietly.

Danny nodded and told Kay what he had learned.

"He says the Grover boy who gave DeeDee such a bad time at the dude ranch a year ago, was the one who loaned them to him."

"Do you believe him?"

"I'm not sure anyone else will, but yes, I do believe him. His story has the sound of truth to it."

She finished setting the table, thoughtfully.

"What are you going to do?"

"First I'm going to call his folks and tell them about it. It's a matter his dad should handle."

"It seems a shame to bring them home."

"I know, but if Del and Doug were involved in something like this, wouldn't you want to know about it?"

Danny telephoned Virgil Trumbo at the home where he and his wife and Patti were staying and told him about the radio unit and model airplane motor Gary was accused of stealing. Trumbo was shocked by the charge and wanted to know if there was any solid evidence against his son.

"I don't want to be one of those parents who has his head in the sand and can't believe his kids can do anything wrong," he said, "but to my knowledge, Gary's never taken anything that didn't belong to him. I can't think he would start now."

Danny agreed with him.

"Frankly, I don't believe Gary is guilty, but there's no question about the fact that he had the stolen items in his possession. Mr. King examined the plane at the park this afternoon."

Virgil Trumbo conferred briefly with his wife before telling Danny that they would leave for Rock Point as soon as he could get away.

Gary had an uneasy feeling about his folks' return. In one way he was glad they were coming back. Danny and Kay were nice enough, and he was sure they wanted to help in any way they could, but having his folks home would be different. He *had* to talk to them and find out whether or not they believed him.

In another way, he didn't want to face them. He hadn't actually lied to them—not with words, at least. But he had deceived them. He had let them think he wasn't going to have a model in the contest. He hadn't even let them know that he was able to finish his plane.

He had only done it because Chuck Grover made him promise not to let anyone know about the engine and radio control unit, he reasoned. And because of that, he tried to make himself believe it wasn't really his fault. Still, he could not blame it all on Chuck. He was the Christian. He was the one who had a different set of rules to guide his life. He should have refused to do what the older boy insisted on.

"What did Dad have to say, Danny?" he asked when the phone call was over. "Does *he* think I took those things?"

Suddenly that became more important to Gary than anything else; more important than what might happen to him if the charge against him was proved.

Danny Orlis took so much time in answering that Gary didn't think he heard him and repeated the question.

"Your dad's behind you, Gary," Danny said finally. "Whatever happens, you can count on your folks. But I think you know that already."

Gary nodded. He had to agree with Danny. He had known it was true even before the young flight instructor spoke, but it was reassuring to hear him say so. The affair was tough enough for him to go through, even when he knew that his mother and dad were standing by him and would do whatever they could to help him prove his innocence. He didn't know whether he could take it if he had to face Mr. King and the police alone.

Virgil Trumbo and his wife must have left for Rock Point within two hours of the phone call. They drove up in front of the Orlis home shortly after dinner that evening.

Gary's mother cried a little when she saw him. He felt like crying, too. But he couldn't do that because Danny and Kay were there. After a minute or two, they all went into the living room and sat down. Only then did his dad mention the shoplifting.

"We were sorry to hear what happened this morning, Gary."

"I didn't do it, Dad," he said tensely. "You've got to believe me!"

"We want to believe you, son."

"And we do," his mother broke in. "We know you wouldn't take anything that didn't belong to you."

"But there are some things that concern me deeply," his dad went on. "You did deceive us about the contest and the plane. You led us to believe that you weren't able to finish your model and weren't going to enter the contest. You didn't lie with words, but you certainly did lie to us by your actions."

Gary licked his lips nervously. "I know. I want to talk to you about that. I—I am sorry."

Remorse swept over the boy in a great, engulfing wave. He pushed his fingers through his tousled blond hair. It wasn't that he had just been confronted with what he had done and realized that he was in the wrong. He had been so disturbed by it the night before that he hadn't been able to sleep.

He realized now that much of the difficulty he found himself in could be traced directly to his decision to deceive his folks. If he had told his dad about the engine and the radio control unit, he wouldn't have accepted the fact that Chuck loaned them to him because he liked him. He would have gone to the Grover house and talked with Chuck's dad and would have gotten some answers that satisfied him, or he would have made Gary give the parts back.

Not that Gary blamed Chuck. He was the best friend he had. He wouldn't knowingly have done anything to get him in trouble. But why else would Chuck have loaned him stolen parts?

7

The Charges Are Denied

GARY DIDN'T WANT to go over to Chuck Grover's, but there was no way he could get out of it. His dad insisted that they go and find out who had traded the engine and radio control unit to Chuck.

"It's the only way we can get to the truth of this thing," Virgil had said.

Gary hunched miserably against the door, trying to wish the next few minutes away. He knew things would be all off between him and Chuck from now on. Chuck would never speak to him again. And the worst of it was, he could do nothing about it.

His older friend was not home, however, and his mother said she didn't know where he went or when he could be back.

"I can have him call you if you want me to," she volunteered hesitantly, as though she was afraid to ask them what they wanted. "But he won't be back until late, I'm sure."

Virgil Trumbo scribbled his name and phone number on a scrap of paper and gave it to her.

From Grover's, Virgil drove across town to Mr. King's hobby store. When they were a block from the store, Gary realized where they were going.

"There's no use in going over there, Dad," he said. "This is Sunday. Mr. King's not going to be opened."

"I phoned him, and he said he would go down to the store and wait for us."

"But why do we have to talk to him?"

"He's the one who made the charge against you."

"But he was awful mad." Gary's voice faltered. "He's not going to want to see me, that's one sure thing."

"That's all the more reason why we have to go to him. He's mad at you because he thinks you're guilty. We've got to start with him if we're going to prove that you're not."

Fear crept into the boy's eyes. "Wouldn't it be better if—if I stayed here in the car while you go in and talk to him, Dad?"

"Nothing doing. You've got to go in with me. We're in this thing together."

The store owner came to the door in answer to Mr. Trumbo's knock and opened it.

"I just got here. You're a little earlier than I thought you'd be."

Virgil Trumbo and his son followed the store owner into the office at the back.

"Well," he began, glaring at Gary. "What do you have to say for yourself? Have you changed your mind about telling me the truth?"

The boy waited for his dad to speak, but when he didn't, he blurted his denial. "I have been telling you the truth, Mr. King. I'm going to tell you again that I—I didn't steal from you."

The man's voice was withering. "You don't expect me to believe that, do you?"

"It's the truth!"

"You're not going to get anywhere with me that way, young man. You were caught red-handed. I'm not going to let you lie your way out of it."

"I know how it must look, but I didn't do it. Honest, I didn't."

Mr. King pulled himself erect and directed his attention to Virgil Trumbo. "Your kid still wants to lie about taking that stuff out of my store. What do you have to say about it? Are you going to uphold him in what he did?"

"I've talked with my son at length about what happened," Virgil said. "I can understand why you would think he's guilty. But I know him. He's never stolen anything before, and he doesn't lie to me."

"You're just like all the rest, Trumbo. I catch

their kids walkin' off with stuff, and they think I'm pickin' on their little darlings."

"But I'm convinced that he didn't take anything from your store."

The man's anger flared. "That's the trouble with kids today! Their folks stick up for them, no matter what they do! I haven't caught a shoplifter in the last two years whose parents would believe he was guilty. Well, this time I've got all the evidence I need to prove it. We caught this kid of yours with things that I can prove came from my store. As far as I'm concerned, that proves he stole them."

"Another boy loaned them to him."

"A likely story!" he exclaimed scornfully. "Well, this time we're going to find out whether your kid's guilty or not. We'll let the court decide whether he stole from me or not."

Virgil Trumbo's voice was firm and unwavering. "I know it looks bad for Gary," he said, "and I can realize your position. I'm sure I would find it hard to believe him myself if I didn't know him so well."

Mr. King's temper exploded.

"The trouble with you is that you don't want to believe it! I know kids! I deal with 'em all the time! They're all alike! If they can't buy what they want, they steal it! Well, I'm going to make an example of this brat of yours. He picked the wrong man to steal from this time."

Mr. King turned toward the door in a gesture that was unmistakable. As far as he was concerned, the interview was over. He wanted them to leave.

"I'm going to the county attorney the first thing in the morning, and when the case comes to trial, I'm going to press for a conviction! You'd just as well be prepared for it! The time for making a deal is past!"

Mr. Trumbo thanked him for coming down to talk with them, and they left the store. When they were outside, Gary turned nervously to him.

"Can he do that, Dad?" Concern edged his voice.

Virgil nodded. "He can't see that you are convicted and sentenced, Gary. Only the judge can do that. But he can file charges against you and see that you're tried by the juvenile judge."

"But why would he be so mad at me and so determined to—to put me in the reformatory."

"He probably has a lot of trouble with shoplifters, Gary," his dad explained. "That might be the reason he is so anxious to have you brought to trial. Sometimes this sort of thing can scare other shoplifters off—at least for a while."

They got into the car and pulled away from the curb. Gary knew he was in a mess before they talked with the store owner, but he hadn't realized things were as bad as they were. If Mr. King had his way, he would be put in a reformatory.

As his dad drove home, the boy prayed silently

for help and guidance. He had prayed before, but never with such agony or desperation.

*   *   *

Virgil wasn't able to locate Chuck Grover that night or the following morning before school. He did learn the boy's license number, however, and found his car in the parking lot at Northwest High. He was standing by the car when classes were dismissed that afternoon.

Chuck charged out of the building as he usually did and made his way for his sports car. He was a dozen paces away when he saw that somebody was waiting for him. He didn't recognize Mr. Trumbo, but the older man's presence was disturbing. He slowed his pace uneasily, and for an instant he acted as though he was about to go off in another direction. But he couldn't do that. It was too late. The stranger would only follow him.

He didn't know for sure what the tall, broad-shouldered stranger wanted, but he could guess that it wasn't anything that would be good, as far as he was concerned. People didn't do that sort of thing to bring good news.

"Hi," he said defensively, trying to sound as though he was in a big rush.

"You're Chuck Grover, aren't you? I've been trying to get in touch with you."

"What do you want to see me about? I haven't done anything."

"Your mother told me you would call me, but I didn't hear from you, so I came out to look for you."

Not until then did Chuck Grover realize that he was talking with Gary's dad.

"I don't have anything to say to you."

"But I have something to say to you." As Chuck tried to push by him to open his car, Virgil grasped him firmly by the wrist. "And you're not leaving here until I do."

The corners of the boy's mouth curled insolently.

"Okay. Let's have it! I suppose Gary tried to tell you that I got that engine and set of radio controls for him."

"How do you know what he told me?"

"I ought to know! He's been blabbin' that story every place he goes to anybody who'll listen to him!" Anger twisted Chuck's face. "I tried to help the kid with his model plane because he's younger than the rest of us and doesn't know anything. I felt sorry for him and tried to give him a hand, but this is the thanks I get."

Virgil Trumbo's gaze bored intently into the boy's. "Why don't you start at the beginning, Chuck, and tell me exactly what happened?"

"Ask your kid! I've got nothing more to say. I try to be a good guy and what thanks does he give me? He tries to get me into a jam to save his own neck!"

Virgil Trumbo continued to press Chuck for

more information, but he would say no more. "I've already told you everything I know. But I can tell you this much! I'm sorry I ever saw that brat of yours!"

Gary was waiting for his father when he came home, and met him in the yard.

"What did you find out, Dad? Was Chuck mad because I told you he loaned me the stuff?"

Virgil's eyes narrowed questioningly. He couldn't quite understand his son. Gary was facing trial for shoplifting, and he was concerned that the boy who got him into the mess might be mad at him.

"He denied everything," he said, going into the house. "He claims he helped you because he felt sorry for you and that you thanked him by taking advantage of him."

Gary winced.

"I knew he'd be mad about it," he said. "I just knew he'd be mad."

❋   ❋   ❋

Danny Orlis phoned Trumbo before they had their devotions that evening to see what they had found out from Chuck Grover. Danny tried not to let his friend know, but he was quite disturbed about it.

Doug read the concern on his face as he returned to the table. "What's the matter? Aren't things going well?"

Danny shook his head. "Chuck denied everything. He claimed that he helped Gary with his model and in return Gary accused him of having loaned the parts to him."

"That's about what you could expect of that character," Del put in.

*   *   *

The day after Mr. Trumbo talked with Chuck Grover, he went in to see the county attorney. The lawyer was pleasant and understanding, but he did not have good news for the missionary.

"King was here just a few minutes ago. I'm surprised that you didn't meet him in the hall. He signed a complaint against your son."

Virgil Trumbo had expected such. He supposed he would have done the same thing if he were the other man.

"I've talked with Gary about what happened, and I'm convinced that he didn't steal those things. . . . I suppose most parents have a tendency to be this way, but I know him better than anyone else and I trust him."

"The evidence is quite conclusive." The attorney had children himself and could understand the turmoil that gripped the man who sat in his office.

"I'm quite aware of that, but it is all circumstantial. Nobody saw him take them."

The attorney shuffled the papers in his hand. He had thought about that, too.

"But the evidence is strong enough to make everyone who has had anything to do with it feel that Gary is guilty. This sort of thing happens often with kids, Mr. Trumbo, whether they have ever stolen anything before or not. They see something they want so badly that the first thing anyone knows, they've picked it up. We deal with it all the time."

"But there's never been any indication that Gary has ever taken anything that didn't belong to him. And he's always been truthful. When he tells me he didn't steal that model engine and control unit, I believe him."

The county attorney leaned forward earnestly.

"I would be quite open to accepting a plea of guilty in the judge's chambers so there would be no publicity. And if your son shows repentance and will give us his word that it won't happen again, I would be in favor of releasing him to you on probation. You see, we're not concerned with exacting society's pound of flesh. Neither am I trying to build a reputation for myself as a tough prosecuter. In cases like this, we want to do what is best for the boy. We have no problems here that can't be handled quite simply."

"But he says he's innocent."

"And you believe him." Only the faintest trace of doubt still remained in his voice.

"I believe him."

The attorney came around his desk and leaned against it.

"In that case I would strongly advise you to fight for him. We're not interested in convicting him of anything. We want only to get at the truth and to give out justice so he won't get involved in anything illegal again."

8

The Attorney's Mistake

DEEDEE DAVIS thought of getting some of the kids to pray for Gary. She called Tina and Letitia and asked them to phone some of the other kids in their youth group. During the week they continued to pray for him. Their prayers were simple and direct, asking God to help the police find the person who was actually guilty so the charge against Gary would be dropped. Christian kids in junior high that Gary scarcely knew stopped him in the hall to talk with him about it.

"We just want you to know that we're praying for you," they told him. "We're asking God to help you show everyone that you didn't steal those things."

Just hearing them talk that way was reassuring to him. He didn't say much to them about it except to thank them. Somehow he was embarrassed to have them talk that way. But it did help. Just knowing that there were some at school who believed in him in spite of the way things looked, was encouraging. It gave him a little confidence that God would hear and answer his own prayers.

Chuck Grover heard about it, too, and labeled it the joke of the year. A couple of days after it first came to his attention, he saw Del and Doug in the hall and stopped to taunt them about it, keeping his voice loud so the kids going by could hear what he was saying.

"What's this about all the prayer for that Trumbo kid?" he asked. "Don't you think a guy ought to have to pay for his sins?"

"That's right," Doug said firmly. "But Gary isn't guilty."

"Don't tell me. Try making the county attorney believe that. He's the one who's going to be trying to send him away for a year or two."

"Gary hasn't been found guilty yet," Del put in. "Don't forget that."

Chuck's face burned. "All this prayer for him is a little late, the way I see it. You should've prayed that God would have kept him from stealing that stuff. There would've been some sense to a prayer like that."

Doug and Del moved closer to the wall to escape the crush of the kids who were surging down the hall.

"He's innocent until he's proven guilty."

"In my book, he has already been proved guilty."

"He's been charged with stealing the stuff, but that's all," Doug said. "We happen to know that he didn't do it, and we're going to prove it before we're through."

Briefly Chuck flinched. It seemed as though the mask slipped for an instant, letting them see what was behind it.

"I suppose you believe that junk about my loaning him that stuff?"

"We sure do," Del exclaimed. "And what's more, you're going to have to answer a lot of questions. That's a promise!"

Chuck Grover snorted angrily. "This is what I get for helping a Christian! I ought to learn. If I ever have anything to do with you 'holy' people, I get burned."

Before they could say any more to him, he whirled and stormed down the corridor, leaving them in the pre-school throng.

"That guy!" Doug exploded in exasperation. "I don't know anyone who can get me uptight any faster than he can."

"Me, too. The trouble is, he knows we don't have any proof, and he probably thinks we can't get any."

"That's where he's going to get fooled! I don't know how we're going to do it, but we're going to get the evidence on him."

❖ ❖ ❖

In spite of the encouragement Gary got from the kids who were praying for him, he was aware of the fact that he lacked any real evidence to prove his innocence. When he thought seriously about it, his doubts came rushing back.

"Dad, do you think it would do any good to go and talk to that county attorney again?" he asked.

Virgil shook his head. "There's nothing we could tell him yet that would help you. We've got to get some proof first."

"But how?"

Virgil Trumbo was silent. He no longer had any doubt of his son's innocence. But thinking about possible proof of it had been keeping him awake at night. He would go over the matter in his mind, detail by detail. There had to be some lead, a tiny chink in the wall of circumstantial evidence against Gary that would lead to a breakdown of the entire case against him.

But there was none—or so it seemed. The more he considered the whole affair, the more frustrated and helpless he felt. Everything they knew about the problem pointed to the fact that Gary had done the shoplifting.

His son grasped his arm in desperation.

"How are we going to prove that I didn't do it?" he demanded.

❊   ❊   ❊

A week more passed before Gary Trumbo and his folks heard anything more about the trial. He pushed the thought of it into the back corners of his mind and almost managed to forget it. Only in the stillness before he went to sleep did he think about it—or when somebody mentioned it to him.

He had even persuaded himself that God was going to work things out so he wouldn't have to go to court at all. He couldn't figure out quite how that could happen, but he began to believe that it was the way the Lord was going to answer their prayers. With everyone praying for him, God *couldn't* let him be punished for something he didn't do.

Virgil Trumbo consulted an attorney shortly after learning that charges had been filed, but he had not said anything to Gary about it. There would be time enough to get his son involved when the trial date was set.

As it turned out, that happened a little sooner than he expected. The county attorney called him at the flight school and told him about it. He knocked off for the rest of the day and was waiting at home when his son came from school. Gary was stunned.

"You—you mean the hearing is going to be held next month?" he echoed.

"That's right. It's set for the eighteenth at four

o'clock." His dad wished there was some way of breaking the news to him in an easier way, but there wasn't.

Gary's pulse faltered, and he licked his lips nervously. "I—I thought maybe they wouldn't go that far with it."

"The charges were filed, so it has to come to court."

Virgil put his arm about Gary's shoulder affectionately. He knew what his son was thinking. "God doesn't promise to answer our prayers in exactly the way we want. He promises to give us the strength and courage to take what comes and to work things out in a way that's best for all of us."

Mrs. Trumbo was crying when they went in to the living room. Gary had to admit that he felt like crying, himself. For a time it seemed as though God had failed him and all the Christians who were praying for him. Now that the hearing was about to be held, maybe he would be found guilty. If so, would he be sent to the reformatory?

He had heard the things his dad said in Sunday school and church more times than he could count. What was that verse? *"All things work together for good to them that love God, to them who are the called according to his purpose."*

That verse was a favorite of certain people in the churches they had attended whenever testimonies

*Romans 8:28.

were given. It was one of those verses that rolled too easily off the tongue, if a guy didn't stop to think what it meant.

He hadn't ever seriously thought about it until right then. He wasn't sure he agreed with it now, or that he could say he honestly believed it. Not the way things had been working out. How could he say that anything good could come from the mess he was in? As far as he could see, it could only mean more trouble.

Now that the date for the hearing was set, Virgil Trumbo and his wife took Gary down to the office of their attorney. He talked with all of them at length about the incident that had caused Gary to be charged with shoplifting. Mr. and Mrs. Trumbo had already told him everything they knew about what had happened, but he wanted to get the information from the boy firsthand. He had Gary go over the events that led up to the contest and the charges against him, questioning him about points Gary didn't think could possibly mean anything as far as the trial was concerned. At last he was satisfied that the boy had told him everything he knew.

"Now, is there anything else you can tell me about it?" he asked gently, but insistently. "There isn't anything you're holding back from me?"

"I've told you everything."

"That's the way it has to be. I don't want any surprises at the hearing. If I'm going to defend you effectively, I've got to know about everything —the good and the bad."

Gary nodded. He had told the attorney the truth, but he didn't think he had been able to help much. "It sure doesn't look good for me, does it?" he asked.

The attorney did not answer his question directly. "There's one thing we should never forget, Gary. In our country, a person is innocent until he's been tried and found guilty in a court of law. That means the county attorney is going to have to prove that you stole the items you're charged with shoplifting. If he can't do that beyond reasonable doubt, you will be found not guilty."

Gary thought the attorney meant that bit of information to assure him, but he wasn't quite certain. The way it looked, they wouldn't have any trouble proving him guilty. He'd be fortunate if he was able to stay out of the training school, or the reformatory, as he had heard it called.

He thought the attorney had finished, but he still had other questions—this time about Chuck Grover.

"Have you talked with him about this?" he asked Gary's dad suddenly. "Do you know how he explains it?"

"He denies everything."

"I'm not surprised. There are some things I'd like to know about the whole affair, and he's the only one who could answer my questions with any degree of authority."

"Couldn't you question him under oath?" Virgil asked. "That way he'd have to tell the truth."

"No," the defense attorney replied, "we couldn't do that. It would amount to our going on a 'fishing expedition.' We suspect some things, but we don't have proof. The judge wouldn't allow us to call him for that purpose." He glanced at his notes once more. "Let's go over this matter again. What day did you say the theft was supposed to have taken place?"

"When I talked with the county attorney, he said that it happened on the twenty-third. That would have been on a Wednesday."

"The twenty-third?" Hope gleamed in Gary's eyes. "Wasn't that the day I was sick and home in bed, Mom?"

His mother spoke up quickly. "That's right, Gary. I called the doctor and got a prescription for you."

The attorney was beginning to get excited. "Now that's the kind of evidence we need. If we can make this fact stick, Gary, we won't have to worry about anything else. This will prove that you didn't take the items."

The boy could scarcely believe that so small a matter could swing the case to him.

"Do you really think so?" he asked.

"I know it will!"

Relief swept over Gary.

When the Trumbo family left the attorney's office, they felt as though the load had been lifted.

"Man, that's a relief!" Gary exclaimed. "I've been real shook up about this whole affair, but we're okay now, aren't we?"

They were still talking about it when they entered the house. They hadn't taken off their coats, however, when the phone rang, and Mrs. Trumbo answered it. When she rejoined her husband and son, her face was sallow and drawn.

"The attorney was on the phone," she said. "He called the county attorney and checked the date the shoplifting occurred. It wasn't the twenty-third. It was the twenty-eighth."

Gary's jaw sagged, and the color left his cheeks. His world crumpled about him. It was all over now! He didn't have any way to prove that he hadn't shoplifted from the hobby store!

9

The Plea

VIRGIL AND GARY went to the attorney's office several times in the next few days to work out the type of defense that would be best. The attorney himself went to see Chuck and talked with the men who worked with the model plane club and a number of the boys who were in it. The attorney had been somewhat pessimistic from the start, and the interviews only increased his discouragement.

"I wouldn't be completely honest with you, Virgil," he said, "if I didn't tell you that things look worse now than they did before. On the basis of the information I've been able to get, I'm very much afraid the judge may find your son guilty. In fact, it is my professional opinion that he would be failing in his duties if he handed down any other verdict."

Virgil stiffened. He knew the case looked black for Gary, but he didn't expect his own attorney to

believe that justice would best be served by finding
his son guilty.

"I take it that you don't believe he's innocent. Is
that it?"

"I didn't say that. I'm quite convinced that Gary
is telling the truth. We do have to face the situation as it is, however. And it is serious."

Gary's throat constricted and he pushed back his
hair with trembling fingers. He didn't have a
chance! That was what the solemn man across
from him was trying to say. He wanted them to
understand that there was no way he could be
proved innocent.

"What can we do?" For the first time, panic crept
into his dad's voice.

"Well, you could have Gary plead guilty. If we
do that, we can then work out something with the
county attorney. There shouldn't be any question
about getting him to go along with a recommenda-
tion of probation."

Virgil didn't want his son to plead guilty, and
he said so, forcefully. "He's innocent. To plead
guilty when he didn't do it is as bad as pleading
innocent when he did."

"But, Dad!" Gary broke in quickly.

"We talked this over, son, and decided that we
would fight to prove you aren't guilty."

"I know that, but that was before we found out

how bad it is. If we don't change, I'll be found guilty and will probably go to the reformatory." He was close to tears. "I don't want that to happen."

"Neither do I, but I don't want you to plead guilty when you're not." He turned to the attorney. "Isn't there anything we can do?"

The slight individual behind the desk picked up a pencil and tapped it thoughtfully on the desk top. "There is one thing you can do that might solve our problem. Gary wouldn't have to plead guilty. He could plead no contest."

The frown lines about Virgil Trumbo's mouth deepened. "Isn't that the same as pleading guilty?"

"Oh, no. In the eyes of the court, the defendant does not admit his guilt. He just says that he is not going to defend himself. It really amounts to throwing himself on the mercy of the court."

Hope gleamed in the boy's eyes. "And if we do that, I wouldn't be sent to the reformatory?"

"It would depend upon the judge, but I'm sure he would use some sort of probation. Especially in a case like this, where you haven't been in trouble before."

"What do you think, Dad?"

He expected his dad to be excited about the new possibility, but he wasn't.

"As far as I'm concerned, a plea like that is the same as pleading guilty. Everyone would think you're guilty and that we've chosen this way of getting you out of it." He turned to the attorney. "What do you think?"

"In a way, I suppose you're right. As a matter of record, most of the people who enter such a plea are guilty, but this is one way of being sure that Gary would not be sent to the training school. The decision will have to be yours."

Gary flinched. He didn't know why his dad was so insistent on having him plead innocent. Couldn't he see what would happen?

That evening Mr. and Mrs. Trumbo sat down with Gary and talked at length with him about the attorney's information that he could enter a plea of no contest and throw himself on the mercy of the court.

"We should follow his advice, shouldn't we, Dad?" Gary asked.

"He didn't advise us to enter a plea of no contest. We asked him if there was anything we could do, and he said this was a possibility. We'll have to make up our minds."

The boy hesitated. He knew what he wanted to do, but he could tell that his dad was opposed to it.

"We've got to make up our minds soon," Virgil continued. "The attorney needs time to prepare his case."

"And," his mother put in, "we don't want to do anything now that is going to hurt you in the future. If people think you stole those things, it could hurt your reputation for a long, long time." She was close to tears, but her voice was strong and firm. "We don't want that for you. You're innocent, and we want everyone to know it."

"I don't like the idea, either, but I don't want to have to go to that—that training school, or whatever they call it."

They were still talking when Patti came in to the living room, standing near the door and listening, her eyes wide with concern. "They aren't going to send you to—to any old training school. We won't let them, will we, Daddy?"

"That's right, honey. You'd better go to bed now. It's getting late."

"What's the use? I can't sleep."

Mrs. Trumbo went over to her, putting an arm about her shoulders. "I'll go in with you," she said tenderly, "and we'll pray for Gary."

"We've gone over things so much we're just talking in circles," her dad said. "I think we'd all better stop talking and pray about it tonight. We can decide in the morning. Okay?"

They all knelt to ask God to give them guidance and direction in the matter. It was one of those problems that seemed to have no right or wrong answer.

When Gary looked at his dad's reasoning, he felt that he was right. Why should he risk having people think him a thief when he knew he wasn't. On the other hand, how could he take a chance with a not guilty plea, when even his attorney said things were black for him? When he finally went to his room and got ready for bed, he was still as confused as ever.

He knew what his dad had said about trusting God. He did want to trust Him. He had prayed more in the last couple of weeks than he had ever prayed in his life, and the Lord meant more to him than ever before. Still, he could not bring himself to the place where he was willing to take a chance by pleading innocent.

The next morning at the breakfast table he told his parents what he wanted to do. "If you say I have to plead innocent, I'll do it. But I don't want to." His voice broke. "I know what will happen if I do. They'll find me guilty and send me away. And I couldn't stand that! I want to plead no contest."

Virgil Trumbo sat at the table a long while before replying to his son.

"I feel you're making the wrong decision, Gary," he said, "but you are the one who has to face these charges. We're solidly behind you and with you all the way, but I can understand how you feel. If you've prayed about it and have honestly made up your mind that this is what you want to do, then

it's all right with me." He glanced at his wife.
"What do you think, Gladys?"

She nodded.

Gary smiled his relief. "Thanks. Thanks a lot!"

The Trumbos didn't think they had said anything to anyone about the fact that Gary was going to plead no contest to the charge of stealing the
model plane engine and the remote control unit.
Word leaked out, however, and before long, most
of Gary's friends knew about it. Del and Doug
Davis heard about it from some of the Christians
at school. At first they wouldn't believe it.

"It can't be. We've talked to him ourselves. He's
not guilty."

"That's what he's going to plead, just the same."

"I can't understand it," Doug said. "I've been
sure all along that he was innocent. Now it sounds
as though we were mistaken and he's pleading
guilty."

Del wasn't sure he agreed with his brother. He
didn't know much about courts, but he did know
that Gary was going to have plenty of trouble proving that he was innocent. "He really doesn't have
much of a case," he said. "It might be tough trying
to prove he didn't steal that stuff. After all, they
caught him with it."

"I know they did, but if a guy's not guilty, I
think he ought to fight to prove it. It makes me
wonder if he did steal those things."

Del pulled in a deep breath as he closed his locker and started toward his home room.

"I'm sure he didn't, but I've got to admit that it looks bad."

The Davis boys were not the only Christian kids who were disappointed in the plea Gary was making. Some thought it proved that he was guilty after all. Others decided that he didn't really believe that God could help him. Only a few of the kids who had been very close to him continued to bring the matter before the Lord.

The morning after the Davis boys learned about Gary's decision to plead no contest, they parked in the lot near the high school and walked toward the entrance of the building. They were almost at the front door when Chuck Grover came hurrying up to them.

"Hey, there!" he called out when he was close enough to get their attention. "Wait up a minute, will you?"

They stopped and faced him. Neither of them really wanted to talk to him, but they could not avoid it. He came swaggering along the walk, a smirk twisting his acne-scarred face.

"I've been wanting to talk to you guys."

Neither of them spoke.

A smile tickled the corners of his mouth. "I understand that little buddy of yours is pleading no contest."

"That doesn't have anything to do with us."

"Oh?" His eyes widened. "I thought he was a good friend of yours."

"He is, but the kind of plea he makes is his business."

"You must really be uptight about it. I guess he finally realized it wasn't going to do him any good to keep lying. He wised up and decided to plead no contest."

"We happen to believe that he's not guilty," Del informed him.

Chuck sneered. "I know what you believe, but that doesn't change things. This sort of throws you, doesn't it? And after all that prayer and stuff. Gary must not believe in that God you guys are always talking about. At least he's too smart to trust Him to take care of things for him."

Del and Doug moved toward the side entrance, hoping to get away from Chuck. But he wasn't going to let them go yet. He kept pace with them, lowering his voice, but still talking.

"Did you ever stop to think that he just might happen to know a little more about how he came to get that engine and the radio controls than anyone else does. Maybe he was glad to plead no contest. It's a nice, sneaky way of getting away from pleading guilty."

"It'll take more than that to make us believe he's guilty," Doug said, surprising himself. He hadn't made up his mind until that moment that Gary was innocent. "We've known that kid since he moved here. He's not the kind who'd steal anything."

The Davis boys expected Chuck to continue his sneering attitude toward Gary, but unexpectedly his entire manner changed.

"I can't see why his old man has been so uptight about this. All Gary had to do was plead guilty. This is his first offense. The judge would be sure to put him on probation. All he'd have to do would be to go down to the court house once a month to report to the probation officer and stay out of trouble. It wouldn't be any big sweat."

Del paused near the doorway and moved to one side so the other kids could hurry past while he and Doug talked with their companion.

"It all depends on how you look at it," Del reasoned. "Sure, he probably wouldn't be sent to the reformatory, but a lot of the people who know him would believe that he stole the stuff. He would be creating a reputation for himself that would take years to live down. His dad is convinced that he's innocent. That's why he doesn't want him to plead guilty."

Chuck squinted at him. "So that's why they came up with this no contest stuff. Pretty neat. There's no risk, and he can always claim that he didn't do it. That's what I call using the old bean."

"You've got it all wrong," Doug replied. "Mr. Trumbo doesn't want him to use that plea. He would like to have him plead innocent."

The other boy snorted his derision. "It's a good thing somebody in that family's got some sense, that's all I can say. I never heard of anything so stupid."

10

The Plea Is Changed

A CHANGE HAD COME over the senior high group at church when Elsie Powell made a decision to walk with Jesus Christ. The kids, sparked by Letitia Warren, showed a new boldness in sharing Christ with the guys and gals in school. Although Gary was not yet in their age group, he, too, had become increasingly concerned about his friends. He was particularly interested in talking to Tom Springer, who had a couple of classes with him.

Practically since they had moved to Rock Point, Gary had been praying for Tom, except for that period when he was so concerned about his own problems that he wasn't able to think about anything else. Now that the matter of his plea to the charges that had been brought against him was settled, he turned his attention back to his classmate and neighbor.

The opportunity for him to talk with Tom about his personal relationship with Jesus Christ came about so unexpectedly that he was scarcely prepared for it. They left their last morning class at the same time and started for the lunchroom together.

Tom talked with him so casually that it was only natural that they would sit at the same table. Gary tingled with excitement. This was the first time that Tom had shown any interest in him.

"You were pretty smart to plead no contest in that charge against you," he said. 'We were talkin' about it at home last night. My old man says they hardly ever throw the book at a guy who makes a plea like that."

"It sure took a load off me, I can tell you that. I was beginning to think they'd send me away for sure."

"Yeh, it was tough your gettin' caught the way you were. If you'd come in with us guys that wouldn't happen. We know the ropes."

Gary winced. Tom thought he was the same as he and his friends. And nothing he could do right then would make him think differently.

He bowed his head and prayed in silence, not only asking God to bless the food, but somehow to provide an opening so he could talk to Tom about his relationship with Jesus Christ. That would show him he wasn't like the gang he ran around with.

Tom saw that he was praying and frowned in

disapproval, but he did not voice his feelings about it. As soon as Gary finished, however, Tom began talking about other things with a determination that he was going to control the conversation.

Gary was concerned. In a few minutes they would be going to their home room for their after-noon classes, and he still had not talked with Tom about Christ.

"How about coming to the youth meeting with me at church Sunday night?" he blurted suddenly. That wasn't really sharing Christ with Tom, he knew, but it was better than saying nothing.

Tom squinted at him. "Why would I want to go there?"

"You'd really like it. We have great times to-gether."

Gary felt Tom's scorn and wished he hadn't said anything, but now that he had, he had to continue. There was no way in stopping.

"You can go with me."

"Why should I?" Tom blurted.

"What do you mean?"

"You know what I mean. That religion of yours can't be very much if it doesn't keep you from stealing!"

"But I didn't take those things!" His voice raised indignantly. "I'm giving it to you straight. I didn't take that stuff!"

The other boy stood, looking down at him. "Oh,

sure! Sure! That's why you didn't plead not guilty!"

The school day dragged endlessly for Gary. He went through the motions of going to class as usual and working on the next week's assignments, but he could not keep his mind on what he was doing. When the bell ended the afternoon's classes, he had accomplished little.

He could still see the scorn in Tom's eyes, and could hear the bitter accusation. Tom reasoned that he must be guilty or he would not have pleaded no contest.

It was just as his dad said it would be. People would believe that he was guilty. This, however, was worse. It was also ruining his testimony. Tom wouldn't pay any attention to what he said for Christ because he thought he was a phony. He wondered if everybody in school felt the same about him as Tom did. Maybe everybody in town had the same opinion.

When classes were over, Gary slipped out of the building as quickly and inconspicuously as possible and made his way home. He didn't want to talk to anyone. He didn't even want to talk with anyone at home, but his dad was there and saw that something was wrong.

"What's happened, Gary?" he asked.

The boy took off his jacket and hung it in the hall closet without answering.

"Would you like to tell me about it?"

He hadn't thought he wanted to say anything, but now that the opportunity presented itself, he went over and sat down.

"Something happened today that really shook me up," he began. He went on to tell about praying for Tom and finally managing to ask him to church with him. "But he wouldn't even let me get started! He said he didn't think I was any different than the guys he runs around with, that walking with Jesus Christ didn't mean very much if I would steal!" Frustration and bitterness marred his voice.

Virgil had been expecting reactions like that. There were always those who enjoyed pointing at Christians as the reason they didn't want to put their trust in Jesus Christ themselves.

"You told him you weren't guilty, didn't you?"

"Sure I did!" He exploded harshly. "But he wouldn't believe me! He said that if I wasn't guilty, I would plead not guilty at the hearing!"

"I see." This, he hadn't expected, at least not from the kids Gary went to school with. He supposed it was the reaction that came from their parents.

"But that doesn't have a thing to do with it, Dad! You know that. I decided to plead no contest because we—we can't get any proof that I'm not guilty that would hold up in court." The distraught boy pulled in a deep breath. "The more I talked to

Tom, the more he said about it. He's sure I stole those things and chose this way to get out of it without having to go to the reformatory."

"That's one of the things we'll have to face," his dad told him. "Quite a lot of people believe a plea like that is made in an effort to get a light sentence or a fine for someone who is actually guilty."

The boy fought to keep back the tears. "It's bad enough to have them think I'm a thief, but I'm ruining my testimony, too. Did you ever think of that, Dad? It could be that I'm actually keeping Tom from turning his life over to Jesus Christ."

Virgil moved uneasily about the room.

"The question is," he replied, "what are we going to do about it?"

Gary had no answer for him. The plea he had decided to make was the safest for him. But what about his witness for Jesus Christ? Was this going to be the way things would be every time he tried to share his faith? Was his tongue going to be completely stopped because of a plea of no contest? If it was, the price to pay was terrible.

He left the living room and went into his bedroom, where he closed the door and knelt to talk with the Lord about it. He asked God to help him to witness effectively and to work in the hearts of those he wanted to talk to so they wouldn't think he was a phony. All the time he prayed, he was thinking only of one thing. The trouble was being caused by the fact that he didn't really trust God. He had been praying that the Lord would prove him innocent. And many Christian kids had been praying for him, too. Still, he hadn't trusted God to work things out. Because the evidence against him looked so black, he assumed that the Lord could not handle the matter. So he chose the safe way. He was getting exactly what his actions asked for. Even nonbelievers knew what he should have done.

Then he realized that he could not allow the no contest plea to stand. He went into the other room where his folks were sitting and told them he had made a new decision.

"I've been doing a lot of thinking since I talked with Tom. And tonight I've been asking God to guide me."

"Yes?"

"I'm not guilty of stealing the model plane engine and radio control unit, and I'm not going to let people think I am guilty by pleading no contest. I want you to call the attorney and tell him I've decided to change my plea to not guilty."

His mother gasped. "But, Gary! We may not be able to prove that you're innocent!"

"I know, Mom. And to tell you the truth, it makes me sick inside just to think what might happen to me if I am found guilty. But, when I was praying just now, it seemed as though God was asking me why I didn't trust Him. I know how hopeless everything seems, and I'm just as scared as ever, but I'm going to plead innocent and trust the Lord to—to help me prove it."

Mrs. Trumbo started to cry, but Virgil went over to Gary and put a hand on his shoulder. "I'm proud of you, son. I think I'm more proud of you now than I've ever been."

"So am I," his mother broke in. "But how are we going to prove he isn't guilty?"

At the moment there was no answer to her question. Virgil wished desperately that he could assure her that their son would be proved innocent, but he could not.

"We're going to have to trust God to help us," he said firmly. "And He will!" Confidence rang in his voice. "He is going to honor Gary's courage in pleading innocent. I know it!"

*   *   *

Del and Doug had difficulty in understanding why Gary had decided to plead no contest previously. They had even more trouble understanding why he made the change. They discussed it with Danny and Kay at the dinner table.

"Why would he change his plea?" Del asked. "Have they found some new evidence to prove that he's innocent?"

"No," Danny said. "I talked with Virgil about it for quite a while this morning. Gary is the one who changed his mind. He tried to share his testimony with some neighbor kid at school, and the guy wouldn't pay any attention to him. He said being a Christian must not mean anything in a person's life or Gary wouldn't have stolen those things from the hobby store. He figured a plea of no contest was the same as guilty."

The Davis boys were both surprised when Gary would take such a strong stand, especially when the same circumstantial evidence was still stacked against him.

"Man, that's great!" Doug said.

"It sure is. That little guy's got a lot of nerve."

"I think it's closer to the truth to say that he's got a lot of faith in the Lord Jesus," Danny said.

11

Chuck Denies Everything

FOR SEVERAL MONTHS there had been talk of organizing a singing group among the kids in the junior and senior youth groups at church. Once they got started singing, they were surprised at the number of requests they received to give programs in the surrounding area.

They had a unique way of making the program more than an evening of entertainment. Midway in the concert they left the platform and went into the audience, shaking hands as they sang. Following that number was a brief intermission. The kids used it to share Christ with those who came to hear them sing. Then when the concert was concluded for the evening, they again scattered through the crowd, talking personally with those who seemed interested. Half a dozen had made decisions to walk with Jesus Christ as a result of those concerts during the first six weeks. Many others who had been out of fellowship with the Lord, confessed their backsliding and came back to Him as a result of those sharing sessions.

The excitement of the group had always been high, and it continued to grow. "It's great to be able to sing in churches the way we do," Doug said at one of the meetings of the group, "but there's something that really bugs me. The guys who need Jesus the most aren't in church. The way things are now, they'll never hear us."

Before they dismissed that night, Tina and Dee-Dee were appointed to see the owner of the Hitching Post about getting something going after the next baseball game. They came home the following afternoon, ecstatic about the reaction they had gotten. The owner of the little eating place was open to having them give a program. He had noticed the difference in the Christian kids who came into his place and said he was glad to do anything that would help the others to be like the Christians.

Gary had been singing with the group in spite of the charge against him, but he wasn't sure he wanted to be in the group when they gave their program at the Hitching Post.

"You know what they're going to say, Dad," he explained. "The kids will give me as bad a time as Tom did."

His dad did not agree with him, however. "You've been accused of something you didn't do, Gary," he replied. "That could happen to anyone.

And you're to be considered innocent until you've been proved guilty. There's absolutely no reason for you to stay home because of it unless the leaders think you should."

"They feel the same as you do. I'd like to go with the kids and sing, but I don't want to keep someone from becoming a Christian, either."

They all went to the baseball game that Friday evening, but Del and Doug scarcely saw any of it. In an hour or so, they kept thinking, they would be at the Hitching Post, telling the kids there what Jesus Christ had done for them and that they too should confess their sin and ask Christ to give them new lives.

Gary had a ride home from the eating place, but not from the baseball field to the Hitching Post. Doug saw him and invited him to go with them. He was as disturbed as they were.

"I sure hope this goes okay," he said.

Doug Davis cleared his throat. "You can say that again."

"I've been asking the Lord to help me say just what I should. Dad says He will, but I feel sort of funny about it anyway."

They had a little difficulty in getting a parking place, and everyone else was at the cafe when they got there. Stan had just made the announcement that the group was going to give a program and had turned the meeting over to Bill Anderson, who was serving as the master of ceremonies. Bill announced the number, and they began to sing.

Del, who was standing on one end, looked down at Chuck as the music stopped. He and four of his pals were sitting in the big corner booth, grinning widely.

"Hey, Stan! What're you going to do now?" one of the group called out to the manager. "Are you getting religious and starting to pass the collection plate?"

Chuck's buddies laughed uproariously as though it was the funniest joke they had ever heard. A few others joined in the laughter.

Bill Anderson announced the second number, and they began to sing. Chuck and his friends didn't quiet down as they had at first, but continued to laugh and talk loudly. When the number was finished, Elsie Powell got up. She had never spoken before a crowd and was so frightened her voice trembled.

"I wish I could tell you how wonderful it has been since Jesus Christ took away my guilty feelings and gave me a new life."

"Hear that, Chuck?" One of his pals broke in loudly, so everyone in the building could hear, "Maybe she felt guilty because you broke up with her."

Chuck's flashing eyes warned him to silence.

"Yeah, Chuck!" Somebody else exclaimed from

across the aisle. "What do you mean breaking up with her and getting her so uptight she has to go religious on us?"

The Grover boy's cheeks were scarlet. "Shut your big mouth!"

One of Chuck's friends half stood and directed his attention to the gang from the church. "Why don't you let us hear from the little jailbird?" he demanded. "Maybe Gary Trumbo's got a confession for us!"

Laughter tittered across the crowd.

"Yeah, he's the one I'd like to hear from. He ought to have some good stories to tell."

"Come on, Trumbo!" somebody else chimed in. "Tell us how you got forgiven for all that shoplifting you've been doing."

Tears came to Gary's eyes.

By this time Chuck Grover was squirming uneasily.

"That's right, Trumbo!" another boy said. "Tell us all about it!"

The youth pastor got to his feet and started up to the microphone. He didn't like to put the kids down, but he could not allow them to continue tormenting Gary that way. Before he could speak, however, Chuck Grover slammed his water glass savagely to the table.

"Shut up, will you?" he rasped.

His companions stared incredulously at him.

They could not understand what had happened that would cause him to defend the missionary's son.

"What's with you?" the one who spoke first demanded.

Chuck jumped to his feet, eyes blazing as he stared down at them. "Just lay off the kid!" he ordered angrily. "I don't want to hear any more talk like that. See?"

His outburst stunned them all to silence. Elsie Powell, who had started to give her testimony, felt the words clog in her throat. One of Chuck's friends swore, bewildered.

"I sure don't get it. You act like he's a real buddy of yours."

Chuck had no answer for him.

"Come on," he rasped. "If they're going to turn this crummy joint into a church, it's time for us to get out of here."

He stormed across the floor and out the front door, slamming it behind him. His companions straggled after him.

Chuck Grover's outburst was so unexpected, it stunned everyone in the Hitching Post who knew him. For half a minute, there was no sound at all. Then the youth pastor broke in to announce another number.

"Bill, I think we ought to sing again before we hear what Elsie has to say."

The kids seemed to enjoy the program in the Hitching Post. They clapped for the music and were quiet and attentive while members of the group gave testimonies. Del and Doug could remember little of what happened after Chuck Grover blew up, however. They discussed it at length on the way home.

"One minute he was making all kinds of fun of us," Del said. "The next he freaked out. I don't get it."

"And did you notice what ticked him off? It was when those guys who were with him started razzing Gary. I thought he would join in with them, but instead he blew his cool. I don't see what got into him."

"Nothing that has anything to do with Chuck Grover makes any sense."

Doug was glad Gary had someone else to go home with when the program was over. He thought that he and Del should go by the Grover house and talk with Chuck.

"Why do you want to do that?" Del asked uneasily. "Don't tell me you're getting lonely for that character."

"Not exactly. But I've been doing a lot of thinking since he let loose in the Hitching Post. He must like Gary a lot, or he wouldn't have come unglued the way he did. If we go over and talk to him tonight, maybe he'll decide to tell the county attorney that he loaned Gary those things and get him off the hook."

Del said he didn't believe Chuck would do anything like that. They had never known him to do anything for anyone else since they had lived in Rock Point. But then they had never known him to defend anyone, either, the way he had defended Gary at the Hitching Post.

"I guess it won't hurt to try."

They were half a block from the Grovers' house when they saw Chuck turn into the driveway and stop.

"Step on it," Doug said, "and we'll catch him before he gets inside."

The other boy was already on the porch when they pulled into the drive. He saw them, however, and came back to their car.

"What do you guys want?" he demanded, surly and belligerent.

"We thought we'd drive by and talk with you for a couple of minutes," Doug said, trying hard to keep his voice calm and pleasant. It wouldn't do to antagonize Chuck now. Nothing could be gained by making him mad.

"I don't care to talk to you. Now, what do you think of that?" He swore angrily.

"We wanted to tell you that we appreciated what you did for Gary tonight. Things were really getting sticky for him."

A strange expression glittered in his eyes. "Don't come to me about Gary Trumbo!" he exploded. "If it wasn't for that stupid religion of his, he wouldn't be in the mess he's in. It's all his own fault!"

"I wouldn't say it's his own fault, Chuck," Doug went on. "Gary tells us that you loaned him the motor and the radio controls. He swears that he didn't steal them."

"And we believe him," Del put in.

"Oh, you do, do you?" Chuck swore again. "Well, he's lying."

"The people who know him best say that he doesn't lie," Doug countered. "But you don't believe what you just said, do you?"

By this time, Chuck Grover was furious. "It so happens that I don't lie, either. Why should I lie about something like this? If I loaned him those things, don't you think I'd say so?"

"Would you?" Doug asked quietly.

"I don't have to stand out here and talk to you two! I've had it with Gary and both of you, so split!"

He spun and stormed into the house, leaving them alone.

Del turned to his brother. "How about it, Doug? Do you still think it did any good to come over here and talk to him?"

Doug Davis was deeply disturbed. For some reason he had been so sure they ought to go over and talk to Chuck, that doing so would help Gary to prove he wasn't guilty. But it hadn't done anything at all. Even if he knew something, he wasn't going to use it to help Gary Trumbo, that was sure. They had just as well have saved their time.

And the hearing was scheduled for the next Monday afternoon at three o'clock.

Doug prayed for their young friend until, exhausted, he went to sleep.

12

The Confession

As far as Del and Doug were able to determine, the Trumbos had been able to come up with no new evidence to refute the charges against Gary. It sounded as though the attorney was going to have to base his case on Gary's reputation, trying to prove that he wasn't the kind of a boy who would steal anything, regardless of how badly he wanted it. Danny was to be one of the character witnesses.

"What do you think's going to happen at the hearing this afternoon?" Del asked at breakfast that Monday morning.

Danny didn't know what to say. He was more concerned for Gary than was comfortable to admit.

"I wish I knew. I'm convinced that he didn't steal that stuff, but unfortunately, about the only thing that will count in the judge's chamber is what we know. I know Gary to be a truthful, obedient

117

Christian lad, but I couldn't swear that he didn't do it."

Doug wanted to know if he and Del could go to the hearing.

"I can see why you'd both want to be there, but I'm afraid this is one case you wouldn't be permitted to listen to. It's a juvenile case, and it will be heard in the judge's chambers. It isn't open to the public."

"But we're not the public. We're friends."

"I know, but the judge won't look at it that way. No one other than the people directly involved will be permitted to attend."

Although the hearing was scheduled for four o'clock that Monday afternoon, it was almost four-thirty when it got started. The judge was busy with other matters, and they had to wait until he was free.

It was obvious from the first that the case was not going well for Gary. The store owner had a clerk and two other witnesses who had seen him in the hobby store a number of times looking at the engine and the radio control unit.

"I want to call it to your attention, your honor," the county attorney said, "that the items he was looking at so longingly are the very same that were stolen."

It was also stated that he had tried to make a deal to pay for them by the month, an arrangement which Mr. King refused. "I don't make a habit of allowing minors to open charge accounts," he had testified.

Still others gave the information that Gary had not brought his model plane back to the club meetings after he mounted the engine and controls in spite of the fact that he was urged to do so on several occasions.

The defense attorney had a boy testify that Gary had told him he planned on bringing his model to the next meeting but had forgotten it. Their case had been damaged by such testimony.

The judge seemed to pay some attention to the character witnesses who came to speak for Gary, but it was apparent that he wasn't swayed enough to rule in the boy's favor. That was evident as he heard one witness after another. He was listening to the concluding statement by the county attorney when there was a disturbance in the hall. The noise was so abrupt and compelling that the proceedings choked to a halt. Before the judge could speak, the door flew open and Chuck Grover charged in, his face white and drawn.

"I don't care if a hearing is going on!" he exclaimed to the bailiff. "I've got to talk to Judge Baker!"

The judge rapped sternly on his desk with his gavel. He had been a judge for more than twenty years and ruled his court with an unbending will.

Now it had been disrupted, and he could not permit that.

"Bailiff! Take this young man out before I charge him with contempt!"

The boy was so disturbed that he didn't even hear what the judge was saying. "Judge! I've got to talk to you!"

The bailiff grabbed him and held his arms tightly to his sides. He would have forced him from the office had Chuck not shouted again.

"Gary didn't steal those things!"

Then the full import of what Chuck was saying came to Judge Baker.

"Let him approach the bench, Bailiff."

When Chuck came closer, the judge spoke to him. "Perhaps you had better tell us what this is all about." He looked up. "This hearing is adjourned for fifteen minutes."

Although stopping a hearing in such a way was highly irregular, the county attorney did not object. He was as concerned about getting at the truth as anyone else in that large office.

"I'm going to ask all of you to leave except the attorneys and this young man." Then Judge Baker addressed himself to Gary. "The bailiff will call you when we are ready to resume the hearing."

Gary left the office with his parents, eyeing Chuck Grover questioningly as he did so. He couldn't quite figure out what was taking place.

Most of the evidence had been presented. In fact, he thought the trial was about over when Chuck had come rushing in and the judge had adjourned it. It didn't make sense.

"What's going on, Dad?" he asked when they were out in the corridor.

Relief marked Virgil's face.

"I don't know for sure, Gary, but whatever it is, we're seeing God's answer to our prayers."

Gary didn't see how that could be. He glanced uneasily at the closed door once more. He had heard what Chuck had said, and appreciated it, but as far as he was concerned, the judge wasn't going to pay any attention to it.

A few minutes later the bailiff called them back into the judge's chambers. Judge Baker's attitude had changed a great deal in the few minutes they were outside.

"I'm very glad to be able to tell you, son, that we have finally gotten to the truth of this matter," he said. "We know now that you are not guilty. Acting on a motion from the county attorney, I am dismissing the charges against you."

Chuck Grover was sitting on a straight-backed chair some distance from the judge's desk. "But I tell you I didn't steal those things," he protested doggedly. "I wouldn't even have come in here if I figured you wouldn't believe me. I—I got those things from a friend."

Judge Baker answered him slowly. "We're going no farther into this matter now, Charles," he said. "We want to give you a chance to talk to your parents and seek legal counsel."

"You mean my old man's got to know about this?" he demanded.

"Your father will have to know."

Chuck stood and started for the door but the judge stopped him with a word. "I must advise you not to leave town or the jurisdiction of this court until the matter is settled. And if you got those items from a friend, I would strongly suggest that you produce your friend."

Chuck Grover was reluctant to leave the office. He clenched his fists and spun on his heel to go back to the judge's desk. "There's no reason for you to get in touch with my old man or to expect me to," he blurted. "I did it! I stole both of them!"

The judge stopped him quickly. "I must inform you of your rights. You have a right to answer our questions or to remain silent. You also have the right to legal counsel. Anything you say now can be used against you."

Chuck's lips curled angrily about the words.

"Don't give me that jazz." Chuck's lips curled angrily about the words.

"I stole the stuff. I admit it."

"But why?" the county attorney asked. "Why

would you steal them and loan them to somebody else?"

"That's just it. I didn't *give* the stuff to Gary, I *loaned* it to him. I figured on letting him take the risk. If there was going to be any flack, I figured it would be coming in the first couple of weeks, or at least before the contest was over. If there was no suspicion that the engine and radio control were stolen, I'd ask him to give them back to me, and I'd be home free."

At first Gary could not believe that Chuck Grover would have done anything like that. He wasn't telling the truth, even now. He was trying to protect somebody else, he reasoned. But, looking across at Chuck's ashen face and quivering hands, he knew his friend was telling the truth. Gary felt as though something had died within him.

"If that's the case," the attorney continued, "why are you here now? Why didn't you let him continue to take the blame?"

Desperation crowded into Chuck's voice. "That's what I planned on doing all along. But he's such a nice little guy I couldn't let him take the rap for what I'd done. To tell you the truth, I thought I had things worked out so I—I could get him off without getting caught myself. I—" The words trailed away. "I see now how stupid I was."

"I want to thank you for coming here on your

own and talking so frankly to us," the judge said. "We can't make any promises to you, but I do want you to know that your courage and truthfulness will be considered when you come before me again."

The owner of the store came over then and shook hands with Gary and his parents. "I'm terribly sorry I blamed you for those thefts. Will you forgive me?"

Gary's smile flashed. "Sure, I will."

"And I want to ask your forgiveness, too, Mr. Trumbo. I made a terrible mistake."

Before they left the courthouse, the store owner told Gary that he wanted him to have the engine and the radio control unit.

"It's not very much, but I do want to try to make it up to you. You're a fine young man."

In the car on the way home, Gary turned to his dad and mother. "What do you think is going to happen to Chuck?" he asked seriously. "Will they send him to the—the training school?"

"I have a strong feeling that the judge is going to be very considerate. You see, Chuck came in and volunteered the information that you weren't guilty. It would have looked much better for him if he hadn't tried to get himself off at the same time, but I'm sure that what he did will be taken into consideration."

"I hope so," Gary replied. "I'd feel terrible if I thought he was going to be sent away."

Mrs. Trumbo put her arm about him and squeezed him lovingly. "Isn't it wonderful the way God worked everything out? And we were so concerned that you would be punished for something you didn't do!"

Gary was silent until they turned in at their drive and the car came to a halt. "If I hadn't tried to deceive you," he said, his voice choking, "none of this would have happened."

"That's true," his dad answered, "but we all do things we shouldn't. When we recognize that we've sinned and ask God's forgiveness, we are not only forgiven, but we should learn not to do that again."

"Don't worry," Gary said fervently. "I've already asked God to help me to be truthful in my actions as well as in words."

"Then I think this whole affair has been worthwhile," his dad observed. "It's just as the Bible says, 'All things work together for good.' "